FULL
CIRCLE

R.N. Chevalier

SR
Stillwater
River

First Stillwater River Publications Edition

Library of Congress Control Number: 2017949285

ISBN-10: 1-946-30021-7
ISBN-13: 978-1-946-30021-8

1 2 3 4 5 6 7 8 9 10
Written by R.N. Chevalier
Published by Stillwater River Publications, Glocester, RI, USA.

This is dedicated to the love of my life, Donna Chevalier, my wife, and to our daughter, Jasmine Chevalier.

CHAPTER 1

"Captain's log, stardate 30125.75. We are seven minutes away from home. If what Amariah said is true there will be Rillians waiting for our return. With this battleship they will be no challenge, no race in the quadrant will be a challenge."

"Y ou know, honey," Daniel says to Atany, "When we get back to Alliance headquarters with this ship we will all get promotions." His excitement bursting through his smile as he slides his leg into his uniform pants.

"That's it!" She shouts with excitement, smiling widely. "You are a genius." She kisses him, the metal studs in her nipples tugging on the hair on his chest.

"What's it?" he asks with an inquisitive look on his face. "What are you talking about?"

"Never mind for now," She answers as she fastens her bra. "I've got to get to the bridge." She slips into her tunic, fastening the buttons.

The two leave their quarters and head for the turbolift. It takes only a few minutes for them to reach the bridge. They step out of the turbolift to find everyone else at their stations. Daniel goes to his station at the sciences computer while Atany takes her position in the captain's chair.

"Put me on ship-wide intercom," she tells Lieutenant Roeton.

"All set, captain." He replies.

"This is Captain Atany," She begins. "We will be home in approximately two minutes. The Rillians will be waiting for us when we exit the vortex. Our primary focus is to destroy the Rillian forces before they can damage this ship. All stations go to red alert. Tactical, power up all defenses and weapons, Ex Vee pilots, prepare to launch as soon as we clear the vortex. Everyone stay on your toes and we'll get through this. Captain out."

The red alert lights glow brightly throughout the ship as the klaxon sounds three sets of three blasts then stops. All the crewmen are doing as ordered, focusing on their various duties and waiting for the peace to come to an end.

The main viewscreen shows a beam suddenly shoot from the bottom of the screen, going up to the center of it, yet far ahead of the vessel. Levi turns to Atany with a look of concern as an anomaly starts to form.

"We're slowing down, captain." He tells her. He looks back at his monitor. "We're stopped." He says.

"That's cool," she says in a matter-of-fact attitude. "As soon as the vortex is stable bring us out."

"Yes, ma'am," he replies.

The spinning circle forms in the middle of the screen, growing larger by the second. It is followed by the second spinning spiral, opening a hole filled with stars. In less than a minute the entire viewscreen is filled with stars.

Amongst the stars are six Rillian battle cruisers. All six ships fire at the mammoth battleship. The crew on the bridge see the six ships fire but feel no impact.

"What happened?" Atany asks.

"The shields absorbed all the energy and returned it as additional shield power."

"Wow!" Atany remarks in awe. "Now that's impressive. Let's see how impressive the weapons systems are." She takes a breath.

"Sacar, Maraka, lock weapons on as many of those ships as you can and fire at will."

The two officers set targeting controls and hit the FIRE button three times each. From each of the two nacelle-like structures on the sides of the ship shoots three volleys of four energy bolts each. Four bolts of energy bolts hit each of the six Rillian ships. The ships rock violently as spontaneous explosions breach their hulls. Another volley vaporizes all six ships instantly.

"That's it?" Atany asks with surprise.

"That's it." Sacar repeats.

"Fuck." She replies with a tone of respect. Hawking acknowledges.

"What do the sensors show?"

"There are no other ships in sensor range." Daniel answers. "We are alone."

"What about planets with breathable atmospheres?"

"Only one," Daniel answers. "Eight point five light years."

"Very good," she says and sits back, deep in thought. A few minutes pass silently. "Set a course for that planet, warp two."

"Done," Levi tells her. "E.T.A. fifteen minutes."

"Lieutenant Roeton, put me on ship-wide again."

"Ready, captain." He says.

"Attention all hands, this is the captain. I want all personnel to report to the hanger deck in ten minutes, no exceptions." She looks around. "Daniel, tie the sensors into a console on the hanger deck."

"Done, captain," he says after a few seconds.

"Let's go," she says to the room as she stands. They head to the turbolift, en route to the hanger deck.

Atany enters the hanger deck behind the rest of the bridge crew. All the other crewmembers are already there. She gathers everyone in a tight half circle. She looks, expressionless, at the twenty-five faces staring back at her. She smiles slyly yet sincerely.

"It dawned on me a short time ago that we, the handful of Alliance officers standing in this room, have been put in a very unique position. We have the most sophisticated, advanced warship in the history of every race in the quadrant." She has everyone's attention.

"We have just destroyed six Rillian battle cruisers, the best class in their fleet, in the blink of an eye. Their weapons impact only made our shields stronger." Several heads cautiously nod in agreement. Atany looks around, her smile getting bigger.

"It seems to me," She says in a softer yet commanding voice, "that we are the most dominate force in the quadrant. We are now the only ones who know this ship exists and how to run her. When we get back to Alliance headquarters with this ship we will probably all get promotions and reassignment." Everyone acknowledges those facts. Atany looks around at the crewmembers in front of her. She smiles.

"How many of you want to leave this ship?" She asks. Everyone answers the way she had hoped. Not one of the crew has any interest in leaving the Tartarus. She smiles widely at their loyalty.

"I propose to all of you that we stay on board, recruit more crewmembers and collect profit worthy of our vessel. Anyone disagree with that mission statement?"

"Great idea!" Comes from the small crowd, in between the cheers.

"We're with you, captain!" Comes from another crewmember. Everyone starts applauding as the cheering gets louder. Daniel and Fental look queerly in agreement. Hawking looks confused.

"We will be in orbit around a small, habitable planet within minutes. When we arrive we will set up a land-based headquarters. After that we will recruit new crewmembers. Everyone here will be promoted up one grade." She tells them with a smile. The cheers and adulation continue.

"Settle down." Atany says with a giggle. The room quiets down and she continues, "I must warn all of you that our objective will be met with resistance. It may get messy. We may have to fight against our Alliance brothers. Is everyone okay with that?" Everyone agrees, some reluctantly.

"Return to your stations." She tells her crew. "We'll have more details within the hour." An alert notification sounds on the panel Daniel tied into the bridge computer. He and Atany approach the panel and investigate the sound. After several seconds they return to the group.

"We are now in orbit above the planet. Break into pairs and search the ship for materials and supplies we can use on the surface. Let's get our home base set up and get some profit." Everyone acknowledges with a cheer and head to their assigned stations. Atany, Daniel, Fental and Hawking silently walk toward the turbolift. The door opens and the four enter.

"What the fuck is going on, captain?" Fental asks angrily.

"This morning I had a massive realization and decided to do something about it." She explains. "I know it's a lot to take in but when you think about it, you'll see where I'm coming from." They remain silent. The door opens to the bridge and they exit.

The four assume their stations. They are the last of the bridge crew to get back. Everything stays quiet for about forty-five minutes.

"Jullian to bridge." Fills the room.

"What's up, Jullian?" She asks.

* * *

"We found a storeroom several decks above the hanger. The Forzak must have been preparing to colonize another planet. We've got atmosphere control units, power plants and what I think are food processors."

"Excellent." Atany says. "Any building materials in there?"

"None." He answers. "That material must be somewhere else."

"Put me on ship-wide intercom, Roeton." Atany orders.

"Ready, captain." Roeton replies.

"All hands, this is the captain. As you search the ship please notify the bridge when a transporter room has been found. Thanks." She says, pauses slightly then continues. "Jullian, start moving the equipment from the storeroom to the hanger. Load it on the Deliverance."

"We're on it, captain." Jullian announces.

"Let me know when you're finished."

"Will do." He says. "Out."

"Captain," Roeton interrupts, "I've got Lieutenant Merah on the line."

"What is it, Merah?" She asks.

"We've located a cargo bay aft of the hanger. It's full of food and seed."

"Great news." She says. Twenty minutes pass.

"Transporter room has been located on deck fifteen, in the drive section." Roeton tells the captain.

"By who?"

"Ensign Voltarus." He answers. She hits her intercom.

"Great work, Voltarus." She says with a slight elevation in her voice.

"Thank you, captain." Comes from the intercom.

"I need you to get that transporter online and operational. Got it?"

"Got it, captain." He acknowledges. "I'll contact you when I'm finished." The line goes dead.

"Roeton, have all personnel not on duty report to the Deliverance for departure to the planet surface." She instructs. He complies.

"Maraka, you're with me." She says as she stands. He gets up and moves to her side. The two enter the turbolift.

Atany enters the Deliverance behind Maraka. There are fifteen crewmembers on board as well as the equipment Jullian found and the seed produced from Merah's search. Everyone is strapped in and ready to go. Maraka joins the archangels in the back while Atany makes her way to the co-pilots seat.

The interior hanger deck doors open as the ship's thrusters engage, preventing the vessel from dropping onto the exterior doors. The exterior doors open and the Deliverance drops from the Tartarus. After dropping down about twenty meters, the engines engage and the Deliverance streaks into the atmosphere, heading for the ground.

The small transport gets tossed around due to the turbulent upper atmosphere. Even with inertial dampeners the vibration rattles everyone's teeth. It's over in less than a minute.

"Set us down five kilometers up river." Atany tells Ensign Torres, who is piloting the craft, as she points to a large river just coming into view on the horizon.

"I see it, captain." He answers. "We'll be there in a few minutes." He adjusts the heading of the ship to comply with her orders.

In a minute and a half the transport is setting down in a large field, isolated by natural terrain. To the east of this field is the river, a kilometer wide where they are. To the south is a huge forest, blending into the mountain range to the west. These mountains stretch northward several kilometers before winding to the east, ending at the river.

The crew disembark on the alien world, spreading out around the ship. Everyone shades their eyes from their first view of sunlight in several weeks.

"Nice landing spot." Hawking says to Atany. "Natural defenses and a water supply."

"There are also caverns at the base of those mountains." She interrupts, pointing to a spot in the mountains about two kilometers north. "We can use them as storage and protection from the elements."

"Very nice, indeed." He says softer.

The two walk along the river, enjoying the sunshine, fresh air and each other for a few hours. The peace and serenity of the area is overwhelming. The two relax completely, comfortable in their silence, just enjoying their time together. The chirping of Atany's communicator breaks the momentary silence.

"Atany here." She says into the black box.

"Voltarus here, captain. I've got the transporters functioning. I'd like to try with inanimate objects to make sure they are functioning properly."

"I've got the perfect test for you." She says. "Lock on to the atmosphere control units, food processors and power plants in the Deliverance cargo bay and beam them to the entrance of the cave about two kilometers northwest from here.

"Got it, captain." Voltarus says. "Transport in progress." Several seconds pass. "Transport complete." He finishes.

"Excellent." Atany says. "Now beam Hawking and I there." They hear the hum of the transport cycle and, from their perspective, the universe vanishes in a hazy, white light. Several seconds later, the white haze becomes the terrain at the base of the mountain. In view, they see the entrance to the cave as well as the equipment from the Delivery.

"Well Voltarus, we made it in one piece." She tells him through her communicator after she mockingly pats herself down.

"Very good, captain." Voltarus replies.

• • •

"Beam us back, please." She tells him.

In seconds they are back where they started.

"Start transporting supplies from the storerooms but not more than half. Got it?" She tells him.

"Got it, captain." She puts her communicator away.

"Everyone gather around." Atany screams to her crew. They all gather around at the ship's hatch.

"Hoon, Aaron, Nire and Nazay, come forward." Atany says and the four crewmen separate themselves from the crowd. "I need for you four to go to the entrance of the cave at the foot of the mountain and start organizing the supplies and setting up the shelter. We'll beam you up when you're done."

"We're on it." Aaron says.

"We'll contact the ship when we're done." Hoon adds. The four head out toward the cave.

"As for the rest of you, get on the ship." She says with a smile. "We're going back to the Tartarus." Everyone files onto the ship and take their seats. Lieutenant Torres and Captain Atany take the flight controls.

The Deliverance takes off and heads for it's stellar rendezvous. It takes about ten minutes for the Deliverance to stop under the hanger bay. The doors open and the ship gently glides into the bay.

A few minutes more finds everyone back at their duty stations. The bridge crew are running diagnostics, on the systems they can, before they depart for their new mission. The medical staff are inventorying supplies in sickbay while the engineers run diagnostics on the engine systems. Two hours pass without anyone noticing.

"Captain," Roeton says, "Aaron is on the comm. They've completed their assignment and are ready to beam up."

"Good," Atany replies, "Get them up here and prepare for departure."

Roeton passes on the captain's orders. Five minutes pass.

"Set a course for the Rhinehart nebula, warp three." Atany gives the order to Levi, who acknowledges and complies.

"E.T.A. eighty-eight hours." Levi informs her.

"Three days." She says to herself but just loud enough for Dutona to overhear. "That should be enough time."

"Enough time for what?" Fental asks.

"To learn the rest of the systems on this ship." She answers. She sits in momentary silence, an idea forming in her mind.

"What are you planning, Dinema?" Fental asks quietly as professor Hawking and Daniel come over. She looks at the three of them.

"Since it was the Rillians who tried to ambush us, I thought we could repay the favor and borrow the cargo that their transports carry. One of their trade routes passes within a thousand kilometers of the nebula."

"And we hide in the nebula and ambush them when they pass by?" Fental half-asks while finishing the captain's thought.

"Exactly." Atany replies. "The plasma from the nebula will make their sensors inoperable."

"Sounds easy enough." Daniel says in a matter-of-fact tone.

"I have one question." Hawking says then asks, "How, exactly, do we go about hijacking a ship?" The four laugh for a short time but, one by one, loose their grins as they realize the seriousness of the question.

"I think we need to learn some basic functions of this ship." Fental suggests.

"What would you recommend?" Hawking asks.

"We need to become familiar with weapons, transporter control, defensive and tractor beam systems." She answers.

"We know all but the tractor beam systems." Daniel mentions to her.

"I don't just mean knowing the systems, I mean knowing the limits of those systems. We need to test them to their limits so we know ours."

"Very good point." Daniel says.

"Thanks." She replies.

"Well then," Atany jumps in, "Let's start intensifying our training on the systems that we know and find the rest."

Hawking goes back to his station, picks up his pad and starts looking over the consoles to the right of his, working his way to the main viewscreen. Daniel goes back to the science station in an attempt to locate the tractor beam controls. Several minutes go quietly by.

"I've got it." Hawking says at the console to the immediate right of his auxiliary science station. "In here." He keys some controls to activate the console. When the unit comes to life, Daniel notices activity on the console to the left of his science station. He double checks.

"I've got tractor beam controls here as well." He says. He checks the panel and, after a few minutes looks at the bridge crew.

"We've got to activate all the consoles." He begins. "Once all the consoles are active we will be able to determine what does what more easily."

"Once we know that," Fental interrupts, "We can set our people up in key positions to run things quicker and more efficiently."

"Exactly!" Daniel finishes with enthusiasm. Everyone on the bridge starts turning on all the computers that are not currently operating.

"Roeton," Atany's attention turns to her communications officer, "contact Benjamin and have his people do the same."

"Right away." He answers as he complies. It takes several minutes for all of the computers to be activated.

"Sacar," Atany says, "I need you, Hoon and Korah to inspect the weapons systems more closely. I want the specs on every weapon and defensive system in our arsenal." The three acknowledge and begin.

"Levi, I need you, Merah, Torres and Richards to learn every aspect of helm and navigational control." They acknowledge.

"Same thing with communications." She turns to Roeton and Reuben. "You two learn all the nuances of the communications array." They also acknowledge.

Several hours pass as the crew complies with the captain's orders. All the while, Atany is studying the schematics and specs of the ship from a mission operations console against the portside bulkhead.

At the end of three hours Atany heads over and sits in her command seat. She sits there for about thirty seconds, in silence, as she rubs the fatigue from her eyes. She turns to the communications officer.

"Roeton, contact Lieutenant Commander Benjamin and see if his people are finished with their analysis." He complies.

"Affirmative." Roeton tells the captain after several seconds.

"Very good. Tell him to get his ass up here right away." She orders.

"He's on his way, captain." Roeton replies.

"Very good." She responds.

She sits in silence for nearly five minutes when the turbolift door whooshes open. She turns to see Benjamin step onto the bridge. She stands and turns to Benjamin.

"Fental, Hawking, Daniel, Levi, Reuben and Sacar, you're with us." She says as she starts walking toward the chief engineer. Everyone else falls in behind her.

The group, led by the captain, heads down the corridor on the side of the turbolift. Several dozen meters down the corridor, on the starboard side, is a door. Atany keys the controls to open the door and enters the room with the group in tow.

In the center of the room is a huge conference table with twenty chairs around it, one at each of the short sides and nine on each of the long sides. Atany sits at the head of the table while the rest sit on the sides.

• • •

"I would like a report from each of you about your systems. When we're done here we'll all have an equal understanding of all the ship's systems and the basic operations." She explains to them. "Engineering?"

"After examining all consoles in the drive section we know there are two inverted graviton generators that produce a field around the ship that causes the mass of the ship to become zero. With that working the liquid propellant engines can bring us to warp six, easily, maybe even a bit more."

"What type of liquid propellant?" Daniel asks.

"A more refined derivative of quadro-hydrolythium." He answers.

"What the hell is quadro-hydrolythium?" Hawking asks.

"It's a mixture of hydrogen and lythium with a molecular phase bonding agent, in this case, quadrozine."

"What's our fuel status?" Atany asks.

"Our tanks are at seventy-one percent." He answers.

"Where are we supposed to refuel?" Daniel asks.

"We have access to all the materials and there are secondary tanks that will process the raw liquid. There are automated systems attached to conduits that draw hydrogen molecules from space. The quadrozine and lythium are mined in the Danarus asteroid field by the Rillians."

"Ironic, isn't it?" Atany says. "Communications, you're up."

"We've found fifty-seven conventional subspace frequencies as well as twelve channels on frequencies that don't exist in the Alliance, or anywhere in our quadrant, for that matter." Reuben explains. "If we can find extra communications transmitters and receivers, we can put them in the archangel's transport and the XVs and, when we pull off raids, we can communicate without worry of anyone eavesdropping."

"There is a storeroom on deck nineteen, in the nose section. You'll find radio equipment there." Atany says. She notices the inquisitive looks from the rest of her crew. "I was reading the sche-matics of the ship. I didn't locate a manifest yet but the schematics show that storeroom is for radio equipment." She takes a few sec-onds break.

"Helm, what have you got for us?" The captain asks Levi.

"As you know there are four individual seats at the helm sta-tion. There is helm, navigation, vortex control and spacefold drive control. We know how to operate the controls but as far as helm and navigation is concerned my biggest concern is sensitivity. We four need a little hands on to get accustom to her maneuverability and handling."

"You'll all have time to get some fly time before we go to work." She tells him then turns to the other side of the table. "Tac-tical?"

"The nacelle-like structures on this ship are the weapons sys-tems. This ship is equipped with eight pulse phased energy cannons fore and aft. They fire simultaneously or in sequence. The shields are the coolest design. I don't know how they work exactly but they absorb the energy from enemy weapons and that energy is converted back into the shield's strength. There are twelve remote laser turrets on each side of the ship for anything that gets within ten kilometers. With these three systems, this ship is untouchable."

"And last but not least, sciences. Daniel, what's your station like?"

"The science station is very much like our standard sensor array, now that we're able to use our tricorders to tie in and translate Forzak to Utorian. The ship's database is much more vast than our own so I anticipate being able to scan faster and more precisely."

"So, overall impressions?" Atany asks, "In your opinions, with the exception of issues brought up here, do you think we're ready?" All acknowledge with affirmation. She looks around then stands.

"Alright, then." She starts. "Let's get back to our posts and we'll let the helm, navigation and tactical guys get some on-the-job training."

Everyone leaves the room, heading for the bridge. Benjamin gets on the turbolift and heads back to the drive section as the others take up their positions. It takes a few seconds for everyone to get settled.

"Levi," Atany starts, "set a course for the Danarus asteroid field. You and Torres pair up and start working together. Merah, you and Richards watch them. In an hour it'll be your turn to take the reins.

"Right away, captain." He replies. Torres sits in the navigations seat.

"Sacar, you and Hoon start target practice. Korah, Rigel, pay attention. When they switch, you guys switch, back and forth, every hour, until we get there." They acknowledge her orders and begin training, destroying asteroids as they pass them.

From the main viewscreen, the stars start zigzagging from left to right, as Levi and Torres become familiar with the ship's capabilities. The two men put the ship through a series of maneuvers including wide and tight turns, corkscrew twists and even loops.

"Captain." Echoes on the bridge.

"Atany here." She says into her armrest.

"Reuben here, captain. We found the communications storeroom. Not only did we find radio equipment for the ships but we also have several hundred communicators. I recommend we equipped our people with these and ditch our Alliance gear."

"Good idea." She says. "Make it happen. Get the radios for the ships down there and tell Benjamin I want them in all the ships. Give them communicators then bring some to the bridge."

CHAPTER 2

"Captain's log, stardate 30215.35. I continue to record these logs not as official Alliance records but as an accurate history of the future. We are three hours from the Danarus asteroid field. My crew is ready and, even though this ship is over a thousand years old, nothing in the quadrant can match it, or match my power. Next step, ore for fuel, Rillian ore."

"How long before we get there?" Atany asks Lieutenant Merah.

"Three hours at present speed, captain." He answers.

"How long until we reach the Rhinehart Nebula?" She continues.

"Six point five hours at present speed." He answers again.

"Daniel, darling," Atany starts with an exaggerated tone of royalty, similar to old time screen actresses, smiling all the while. The smile vanishes as she continues. "Let me know when we get within scanner range of the asteroid field."

"But of course, my dear." He replies in the same accent she used on him. He buries his face in his monitor, analyzing the data coming from the forward sensor array. Thirty minutes go by with nothing to report.

"I've got the outer edge of the asteroid field, captain." Daniel says.

"Yeah, right." She says with a snicker. "Let me know when you get a reading."

"I'm serious." He says reassuringly. "I'm picking up the asteroid field."

"Stop fucking with me. You shouldn't be in range for another hour."

"Hello…" He says half-jokingly. "Forzak technology."

"That's true too." She says. "Let me know when you pick up transports with the ore we need."

"Will do." He replies.

Twenty minutes pass. Daniel turns to Atany.

"I've got three transports in sensor range. All three are fully laden with quadrozine." He says somewhat loudly.

"Great!" She says excitedly. "How long until we're in weapons range?"

"Two hours and eight minutes." He replies. The excited look on her face fades away.

"How fast are they traveling?" She asks.

"Warp one point five." He answers.

"Helm, if we increase speed to warp four and take an elliptical course to the nebula, how long will we be waiting before those transports get there?" Atany asks Merah.

"We'll get there twenty minutes ahead of them." He answers.

"Excellent. Get us there now. Stay out of their scanner range."

"On it." He says as he manipulates the controls. The massive battleship speeds along at seven hundred and eighty kilometers a second.

"Nebula two minutes ahead." Merah announces.

"Slow to impulse." Atany orders and the streaking stars on the screen become a static view of the local region. Directly in front of the ship, taking up half of the vertical screen space and three quarters of the horizontal screen space, is the Rhinehart nebula.

"Distance?" The captain commands.

"Seven hundred thousand kilometers," Merah answers.

"How far away are the transports?" Atany focuses on Daniel.

"Nearly one hundred million kilometers," Daniel answers.

"Full impulse. Get us in there. We'll have about ten minutes to get ready." She says. The image of the nebula gets visibly bigger as the seconds tick by. In less than ten seconds the ship is fully immersed in the cloud. The visual distortion that ships encounter in the nebula is sporadic and minimal.

"What's up with the sensors?" Atany asks Daniel.

"Don't know how they did it but the sensors are functioning at eighty percent." He answers. "I should have the transports back on my monitor in about two minutes."

"Very good. Now we wait." She concludes. The seconds tick by, each one slower than the last. As the final seconds approach, the crew seems ready to jump out of their skins. The two minute mark comes and goes with no sign of the three transports.

Twenty seconds pass without the ships. Forty seconds pass.

"Here they come." Daniel says after nearly a minute. "There are two." Several seconds pass. "There's the third. Readings indicate they slowed down, now at warp one."

"That should make things a bit easier." Fental comments aloud.

"They'll be in striking range in nine point five minutes." Tactical officer Korah reports.

"Tactical on main viewer." Atany orders. The image on the view-screen becomes a solid blue backdrop with ten black rings expanding evenly outward from a center dot. The center dot has a green dot overlay, representing the Tartarus. Four rings up and at the left edge of the screen are three red dots, representing the Rillian transport ships.

The bridge crew sit silently at their stations watching the three red dots slowly move across the screen. A small rectangular window at the top, center of the screen shows a timer counting down the time until the Rillian ships are in striking distance.

As the ships move closer to their rendezvous with destiny and the timer counts down, the adrenaline starts to pump through everyone on the ship. They sit silent and motionless as the universe revolves around them. They sit waiting until the moment when their actions change their lives forever.

The timer on the screen reads five minutes. Sweat starts to trickle down the captain's face. Nervous glances shoot around the room. Fingers start to tap lightly on consoles.

The timer reads four minutes. Glances shoot quicker. Nervous looks shroud their faces. Nervous energy fills every pore of every member of the crew, not for the morality of their actions but for their actions alone.

The timer counts down to three. Fingers tap on consoles louder. Several crewmen start fidgeting in their seats, the adrenaline rush starting to overwhelm them.

Two minutes left on the clock. Atany stands up in place and slowly looks around the bridge. As the clock ticks down Atany turns to her tactical officers. She walks over to their stations and leans on the terminal.

"We need for you to take out the shields and engines. Each of you pick one. Be careful not to destroy the ships... Not yet, anyway."

"Not to worry, captain." Lieutenant Commander Korah replies. "Rigel and I will cripple them, for now." He smiles at his commanding officer and she smiles back.

One minute left. Atany sits down in her seat, leaning forward with elbows on knees. The clock reads thirty seconds.

"Bring forward thrusters to one half." Atany orders. "Take us out slow. When we clear the nebula, take out the lead and last targets then the center one."

As the ship moves slowly toward the transport's flank the six archangels are waiting in the transporter room, MX-1903 assault phaser rifles in hand.

"Set phasers to level six." Lieutenant Commander Daniel tells his team. "We'll go in teams of two, one in their engine room and one on the bridge. Each transport has a crew of six. There'll be at least two on the bridge, for sure, and two in the engine room. The other two are the unknowns. Stun everyone then stop the ship. Got it?" The group cheers.

"Give me my screen." Atany says aloud and the tactical display is replaced by the space outside of the ship. The cloud-like pockets of gases start to give way to patches of stars shining in a sea of black.

"Tactical, fire at will." Atany says. Seconds tick by as the gases thin out into nothingness. Ahead of them, about thirty thousand kilometers, are the Rillian transports, two close together on the right and one dragging behind a short distance.

"Full impulse now." Atany says and in a second the three ships on the screen start to get bigger very quickly. Then, from the sides of the screen, energy bolts can be seen shooting toward the transports. Three bolts hit each transport. Each ship has minor explosions emanating from different decks.

"Voltarus, Richards, you're up." Daniels tells them and they get on the transporter pad. "Beam them to the lead ship." He tells

Fental, who is manning the transporter. She slides the controls and the two men disappear.

"Torres, Nire, go." He turns to Fental. "Last ship." They beam out.

Daniel motions to Hoon as he gets on the platform. Hoon follows and takes his spot.

"Let's do it." Daniel says and he and Hoon sparkle into nothingness.

The transporter cycle finishes and Daniel finds himself on the bridge of the transport ship. The Rillian captain jumps back in his seat in surprise as his helmsman flies out of his seat, hit by the beam of a phaser rifle.

The captain turns to see where the shot was fired from and gets a boot in the face for his trouble. Daniel executes a perfect side kick to the captain's face and he spins from his seat, landing unconscious on the floor. Daniel heads to the helm station and stops the engines. He takes out his communicator.

"Hoon, Report." He says into the box.

"Hoon here. Three down."

"One left, stay sharp."

"Copy that."

Daniel manipulates a knob on his communicator.

"Daniel to Tartarus."

"Atany here. Report."

"Ship taken. One target unaccounted for. Hoon's on it." He answers. "How'd the others do?"

"All three taken. No lives lost and no one killed." She replies. "Get your prisoners together then notify Fental. She'll beam them to a common area here. Then we'll transport the ore to our storage tanks."

"Got it. Out." He puts his communicator away and ties the two unconscious aliens together. They sparkle into nothingness.

He cautiously makes his way to the engine room, searching room by room, deck by deck, along the way. He meets Hoon on deck four.

"Did you find number six?" Daniel asks.

"No. Did you?" He responds.

"No. Let's get to the engine room and grab the three down there. We'll have them beamed back then we'll go to the bridge. We can use the internal scanners to find him."

"Let's do it." Hoon agrees. They head aft to the engine room.

The two men enter the engine room to find the three men gone, their restraints on the floor where they were left by Hoon.

"What the hell?" Daniel responds with annoyance.

"Damn," Hoon replies angrily.

"Let's get to the bridge and find the missing men." Daniel says. Hoon agrees and they slowly make their way toward the bridge. They make their way up to deck two. The door of the turbolift opens. The bulkhead six inches to the right of Daniel's face explodes in a shower of bright, hot, sparks. Half a second later the sound of the Rillian phaser weapon is heard. Both men drop to the floor.

"Shit!" Daniel; screams in surprise as he heads toward the floor. A slight scream comes from Hoon. Another blast is heard, this time inside the turbolift, right where Hoon had been standing a second ago.

As Daniel rolls to the right, taking cover within the turbolift, Hoon fires his phaser and hits the Rillian soldier. Unfortunately, the shot took half of the Rillian's face and splattered it on the bulkhead.

Daniel lines up a shot and fires. The beam hits the soldier in the chest, sending the Rillian to the floor. The two men carefully stand and exit the lift. Hoon ties the Rillian's Hands behind his back while Daniel checks a few meters down the hall. They clear the deck and drag the unconscious Rillian onto the turbolift. The door closes.

"They've got to be on the bridge," Daniel says.

"They're probably waiting for us." Hoon replies.

"Let's not give them big targets," Daniel tells Hoon as he drops to one knee, lining up his weapon with the door's edge. Hoon drops to his knee, activating the turbolift on his way down.

After two seconds the lift stops and the door opens. Daniel and Hoon look out to see the remaining two Rillians. One is at the helm station and the other is at the terminal to the right of the captain's chair. Both are keying in commands. The archangels fire and the two Rillians drop to the floor.

The Alliance officers rush out to see what the soldiers were doing. They notice that all the computer controls are locked.

"Come in, Tartarus," Daniel says into his communicator.

"Go ahead," Atany's voice sounds from his unit.

"Beam the two Rillians near my comm signal to join their friends. We'll beam over shortly." The two aliens sparkle away.

A moan is heard from the turbolift. Daniel and Hoon go to the lift and pick the semiconscious Rillian off the floor. They sloppily drop him in the captain's chair. A few seconds later the soldier opens his eyes.

"Ah, you're awake." Daniel says with some sarcasm.

"What the fuck is the meaning of this?" The Rillian screams in anger using his best Utorian dialect. "Why did you attack us?"

"Shut up." Daniel says with a slightly raised voice as he sharply smacks the side of the Rillian's head with an open palm strike.

"How do we unlock the computers?" Daniel asks.

"Fuck you!" The Rillian says with disgust.

"No thanks." Daniel answers. "You're not my type." A second palm strike hits the captain's head.

"How do we unlock the computers?" Daniel asks again, with a grin. The soldier remains in defiant silence. A third palm strike hits the Rillian's head. This one is the hardest yet. The Rillian's head sharply snaps to the right, his eyes rolling back in his skull.

"I'll ask one more time." Daniel says, staring intently at the alien. "How do we unlock the computers?" His grin fades away as he raises his hand slowly.

"Access code is T'pa, Klee, two, one, six!" He screams at the Alliance officer. Daniel keys in the commands and half of the computers come back to life. Hoon does the same and the other half come to life.

"Contact the ship." Daniel tells Hoon, never breaking eye contact with the Rillian. "Get us back there."

The turbolift door whooshes open and Daniel steps onto the bridge with Fental. The two take their posts.

Atany's eyes grow wide as a huge grin sweeps across her face. She spins in her seat, wild with excitement. She stares at Hawking.

"Professor, Could I interest you in going over to one of the transports with Fental?" Dinema's face contorts with inquisitiveness.

"For what purpose" He asks.

"Recover any Rillian technology that the Alliance doesn't have."

"It's an intriguing idea, captain, but the technology we possess is far superior than anything they can have that we don't know about."

"It's not for us. It's for insurance." She explains. "You never know when secrets might come in handy.

"Ah," He says as the light bulb above his head clicks on. "I see your point. Very good idea. I think we can do that." He and Fental head to the transporter room, the turbolift door closing behind them. Atany sits back in her seat.

Fental and Hawking materialize on the bridge. All the consoles are still functioning, just as Daniel and Hoon had left them.

They take out their tricorders and start recording everything they see.

"Can you contact the ship?" Hawking asks Fental as he adjusts the controls on his tricorder. "Have them tie the computer to my tricorder and upload this ship's database. He puts his tricorder on the captain's chair and continues to look around.

"All set." Fental tells him. "Upload will take about forty minutes. We need to be back by then.

"No sweat. Let's look around, since we have some time." He suggests.

"Let's do it." She replies with a smile.

"We need to check the medical bay and engine room for any gadgets we could possibly use." Hawking tells her. She agrees and they head down the hall at the back of the bridge."

They stop in the medical bay one deck below. There is one exam bed in the middle of the room with a full body scanner mounted on the ceiling above it. The left wall has a large, flat screen monitor mounted to it, no doubt connected to the imaging scanner on the ceiling. The right wall is bare with only a desk and chair along it. The far wall is made up of shelves and cabinets that store all the medical supplies.

"Grab one of each piece of mechanical equipment you can find." He tells Fental. "I'll start on the left. "You start on the right."

"Okay." She answers as she starts looking through draws and cabinets, throwing things out onto the floor, not caring about the mess. By the time they meet in the middle they've accumulated eleven items to bring back.

They leave the medical bay and make their way to the engine room two decks below. They enter the engine room and find it as bare as the medical bay. There are cabinets along the port and starboard side bulk-heads. The center of the room holds one Dynotherm liquid fueled engine, capable of pushing this ship to warp two point five, connected to the thruster exhaust port. Four conduits run from the top of the engine to the ceiling.

• • •

"I'll check this side." Fental tells Hawking as she points to the right.

"Cool. I'll go this way." He responds as he walks to the left. It takes ten minutes for them to finish searching through the engine room. They've collected another seven items.

They leave the engine room and head down the hall toward the front of the ship. Each room they enter is crew quarters. The last room they enter is the largest of the quarters.

"This must be the captain's," Fental says.

"Looks like it." Hawking agrees. "How long before the upload is complete?"

"About twenty-five minutes." She tells him.

"Good," He says with a smile as he pulls her close, kissing her gently but with authority. Their lips stay locked together as they undress each other. Fental spreads herself out on the captain's bed as Hawking buries his face between her legs, gently rubbing her clit between his lips.

It takes just under five minutes for Hawking to bring Fental to her first orgasm. When her body finishes convulsing she catches her breath.

"I want you inside me," She says with determined conviction.

He pulls himself up so they are face to face, gliding his body over hers. As he slips his rock hard cock into her wet pussy he looks her in the eyes.

Even though Fental's beauty rivals Atany's, Hawking notices one huge difference. He sees sincerity in her eyes, sincerity that makes her some much more appealing. He starts to thrust his cock in and out of her with a single objective, bring her to another orgasm.

They lock fingers as Hawking lifts himself above Fental. Her tits bounce freely in every direction as he slams her pussy. It takes only ten minutes of thrusting while watching the expression on Fental's face brings Hawking to a building orgasm.

● ● ●

As his body tightens, preparing to explode, she feels his approaching climax and her own body explodes in orgasmic ecstasy. They come together while moaning through locked lips. They collapse in a lump of sweaty flesh, remaining there for several minutes.

Hawking rolls off of the former archangel and starts to get dressed.

"We've got to get back to the bridge." He tells Fental.

"Oh, yeah," She says as she rolls to the edge of the bed.

"We still have about five minutes," She says after looking at her tricorder. "Plenty of time," She finishes with a smile as she starts to get dressed.

It takes about three minutes for the two to finish and head out of the cabin. Another two minutes find them on the turbolift, the door opening to the bridge. Hawking approaches the captain's chair and looks at his tricorder.

"Still have a whole minute left." He says. Fental starts to laugh and Hawking joins her. The tricorder beep interrupts their laughter. Hawking picks up the tricorder as Fental activates her communicator.

"Fental to Tartarus, two to beam up."

They go from the transporter room to the bridge. The turbolift door opens and they step onto the bridge, turning to the station Hawking has been using. They place the items on the console as Atany walks over to them.

"I see your trip was successful." She says to the two.

"Oh, yeah." Fental says. "I think we can use some of this stuff when it comes to dealing with the other races."

"Excellent." Atany replies with a smile.

"Captain," Reuben says. "Benjamin reports all the ore has been transported into the storage tanks."

"Great." She answers. "How are we doing with the upload?"

"We finished right before we came back," Fental tells her.

"Beautiful." She says. "Are there any other ships in sensor range?"

"None." He answers.

"Okay, keep an eye out." She says.

"Will do." He answers.

"Store these toys you brought back." Atany tells Hawking. "I'm going to talk to our guests. Fental, the bridge is yours till I get back." She gets on the turbolift.

Atany enters the cargo bay on deck twelve, phaser rifle in hand, to find seventeen very pissed off Rillians standing close together. As soon as the door closes they all start screaming at her at once.

"Shut up!" She screams, pointing the phaser rifle at the Rillians, sweeping it slowly from left to right, threatening all of them at once. The room becomes silent in less than a second.

"That's better." Atany says calmly, with a smile. "I'm only going to say this once. You have two options tonight. The first, join my crew, pledge allegiance to me and my crew. The second, die. What will it be? You only have a few seconds." The Rillians stand silent, ignoring her.

"Don't test me, gentlemen. You will lose." She stands firm. Two of the Rillians reluctantly step forward, not wanting to die.

"Good." Atany says. "Anyone else?" She waits several seconds." Okay, so be it." She hits the button on the communications console mounted on the wall to her right. "Transporter room. Atany here. Beam the Rillians standing together to the lead ship." They fizzle away. She hits the button again.

"Bridge, place a tractor beam on all three ships and jam all channels, I don't want them transmitting." She turns to the two Rillians. "Come with me." The three walk down the hall and board the turbolift.

The three step onto the bridge. Atany takes her seat with the two aliens beside her. She takes a few seconds for dramatic effect.

"I want to show the two of you what will happen if you should choose to attempt escape, sabotage, or you try to hurt any member of this crew, understand?" The two Rillians acknowledge.

"Tactical." She says and gesture to the Rillians to watch the screen.

From both the left and right sides of the viewscreen, a series of focused energy bolts appear, racing toward the Rillian ships.

The two crewmen stare with widening eyes as the bolts get closer. Their expressions turn to horror as the energy bolts decimate the three transports instantly.

"Why did you do that?" The Rillian on the left yells in disbelief. "They were unarmed, defenseless."

"That was to show you the resolve of my crew. One slipup and you get the same thing. Got it?" Her sly grin returns.

"Absolutely, captain." The crewman on the left says.

"By your command." The one on the right answers.

"That's what I thought." She says as she sits back in her chair.

CHAPTER 3

"Captain's log, stardate 30220.02. We have replenished half of our fuel supply. Now we need to find lythium and we'll be done with the Rillians, for now. Our two new crewmen have yet to prove themselves but I feel the time for them to do so is coming quickly."

Atany looks around the bridge in silence. She contemplates the events of the past hour and is trying to decide their next course of action.

"Daniel, anything on the scanner?" She asks him.

"Nothing yet." He answers.

"Helm, set a course back to the asteroid field. Keep the transportation corridor at the edge of sensor range. We need to know when ships carrying lythium are passing. Keep us at one quarter impulse."

"Aye, captain." Merah answers as he manipulates the controls.

Time continues to tick by slowly. There is no sign of any Rillian transports. For an hour there has not been one ship of any kind.

"Transport coming into range." Daniel says after another fifteen minutes. "Make that two... now three... make that four... Yes, four transports in a convoy."

"What are they carrying?" She asks.

"Quadrozine." He answers.

"Let them go." She says. The bridge crew stands down.

Ten minutes pass silently by.

"I've got two more transports in range." Daniel says. "Forget it." He continues after a few seconds. "Fuck!"

"What is it?" Atany asks.

"The lead ship is carrying lythium but the second is carrying quadrozine." Disappointment in his voice.

"Can we try to beam the ore from their holds without them knowing? Hawking asks. "They're transports. I don't think their shields are any match for us."

"That's a good idea." Atany says with surprise. "Why didn't you think of that sooner?" She asks with a smile and giggle.

"Hey, I can't be a genius every second." He says with a smile.

"Fental," Atany turns to her first officer. "Will you handle the attempt? If anyone can do it, it's you."

"I'll give it my best shot, captain." She replies as she stands. "Daniel, I'll need to coordinate with you and Merah." She tells him as she walks to the turbolift. It takes only two minutes for her to get there.

"Daniel, Merah, do you read me?" Comes through the intercoms at the science station and helm simultaneously.

"I read you." Daniel answers.

"So do I." Replies Merah.

"Helm, bring us within transporter range but keep us clear of their sensor beams. Let me know when we're in position." Thirty seconds go by.

"We're in position." Merah tells Fental.

"Stand by. I'm attempting transport." She says. Several minutes pass.

"Transport complete. We have the ore." Fental's voice fills the bridge.

"Confirmed, captain." Daniel says with a smile. "Sensors show their cargo bays are empty."

"Good work, everyone." Atany says. "Fental, get your pretty butt back up here."

"Benjamin, how much more lythium ore do we need?" Atany asks her armrest.

"If what we just got represents a full transport, we need four more ships full." Benjamin's voice echoes.

"Thank you. Out."

Less than a minute later the turbolift door opens and Fental steps onto the bridge and takes her seat by the captain. The room remains quiet as the crew returns to the mission at hand.

As the minutes pass, the crew deals with the normal operational protocols. Systems status reports are reviewed. Information related to the stolen Rillian equipment and database is looked over, the two new Rillian crewmen being instrumental in compiling the information.

"I've got three more transports in range." Daniel says after a forty-five minute lull.

"Cargo?" Asks Atany.

"I'll need a few more seconds." He answers.

"Understood." She replies.

"Lythium." He answers Atany after thirty seconds. "All three."

"They'll be in transporter range in seven minutes." Merah volunteers.

Atany looks at Fental and, without words, the first officer gets up and heads for the turbolift.

"I'll call you when I'm ready." Fental says to Daniel and Merah just as the turbolift door closes. Several minutes later the intercom lights at helm and the science station light up. The two men tie their systems into the transporter control. They are ready to begin the operation.

Unlike other situations, time flew by and, before anyone knows it, the transports are in range. Fental starts beaming the raw ore into the storage tanks and the computer starts the automated process. Ten minutes pass. The transports continue on without any deviation.

"Fental to bridge." Comes from both the science station and helm control. "I've got every kilo of lythium from all three ships." The bridge crew let out a cheer. Fental hears the commotion through the intercom. She heads out of the transporter room and back to the bridge. She steps out of the turbolift to a round of applause from the rest of her peers, including the captain.

"Thank you." She says with a smile and the same old time actress attitude the captain demonstrated earlier. "Thank you. You do love me." She starts to blush as applause turns to solid laughter. She walks over and takes her seat near the captain.

"Helm, set course one, eight, three mark one six, five, warp five."

"Aye, captain," He says as he complies, "course one, eight, three mark one, six, five, warp five confirmed."

The screen becomes streaking stars as the ship attains it's traveling speed of one hundred and twenty-eight trillion kilometers per hour. The captain sits back in her seat.

"What's up, captain?" Fental asks Atany quietly.

"I want a Horatha invisibility shield generator." She replies.

"What are you going to do?" Fental asks. "Just take one?"

"How well you know me." Atany says. "But right now I'm going to bed. I can't remember the last time I slept."

● ● ●

"That sounds like a great idea." Fental agrees. "I think I'll do the same." She says as she and the captain stand. They start walking toward the turbolift together.

"Daniel," Atany turns her head, facing her husband. "The bridge is yours until the next rotation. Tell Lieutenant Commander Levi he has the bridge until I get back. Also tell him to avoid every ship until further notice and tell him I don't want to be disturbed until I get back. And please emphasize 'do not disturb'." She blows him a kiss as she steps onto the turbolift. The door closes with the familiar whoosh sound.

Atany steps onto the bridge with a smile and a warm greeting. Levi sees her and gives up the captain's chair. She takes her seat and greets Fental. She sits back and takes a breath, exhaling slowly.

"Lieutenant Jasmine, are there any Horatha ships in sensor range?"

"None yet, captain." The young XV pilot, now part time science officer, tells her. "I'll let you know as soon as one comes into range."

"Right on." Atany says, still smiling. "Levi, are we in Horatha territory yet?"

"We'll be there in five minutes." He answers.

"Reduce speed to warp one point five." She orders. "I don't want to come up on an unsuspecting ship so fast that they see us." Everyone on the bridge looks at the captain with puzzlement. It takes her a few seconds to notice. She activates her intercom.

"Attention crew, this is the captain. We will be entering Horatha space in several minutes. We are going to find a Horatha cruiser. We are going to board it and we are going to covertly steal their invisibility shield generator." She explains to her crew. "I would like all of the archangels to meet in the conference room near the bridge in ten minutes." She finishes.

"Daniel," Atany starts as the room quickly quiets down. "Can you and your team devise a plan to enter a ship, locate and steal the generator, and get back undetected?" He gives her a troubled look.

"Normally I would say no problem." He starts reluctantly.

"But?" Atany interrupts.

"But, we have two problems." He begins again. "First, we don't know the layout of the ship and, second, we are a seven man team, we'll need to compensate tactics. We'll get it done but can't guarantee complete stealth."

"That's why Fental is here. Before she was my science officer, she was trained as one of you." Atany tells them. Everyone but Daniel looks surprised at the news.

"You don't seem surprised." Fental addresses Daniel.

"I knew there was something different about you when I was training you." Daniel admits. "I had my suspicions but knew I'd find out sooner or later."

"Any problem with me joining your team?" She asks the group while eye to eye with Daniel. After several seconds she looks around at the rest of the team.

"No problem." Voltarus says, along with Richards.

"I'm cool with that." Torres adds, as do Nire and Hoon.

"Welcome aboard, Fental." Daniel says with a grin.

"Let's get this plan devised." Hoon suggests and all agree.

"Good, it's settled." Atany says as she stands. "You seven get a plan together, the sooner the better." The captain leaves the conference room in the direction of the bridge.

Atany, back in her seat for fifteen minutes, is focused on the main viewscreen, lost in thought. An unfamiliar beep from the right catches her attention. She spins to face Lieutenant Jasmine at the science station, filling in for Daniel and Fental.

"I have two energy fluctuations ahead, three million kilometers, traveling at sub-light speed." Jasmine reports.

"Helm, match their course and speed." Atany says quickly and he does.

"Let's make sure they are Horatha, Jasmine." Atany says to the newest science officer. "Keep monitoring those fluctuations. Let me know if and when they change course."

"Aye, captain." She responds. Twenty-five minutes tick by with nothing out of the ordinary happening.

"Captain, they're slowing down." Jasmine says, surprise in her voice.

"Could they have seen us? The captain asks.

"No, I don't think so." Jasmine answers. "We are at a distance almost twice the range of Alliance scanners. I haven't heard that the Horatha have that much of a leap on us technologically."

"Yeah, but with the Horatha, who knows." Atany adds, "Helm, match their speed, let's see what they're up to." Several more minutes pass by.

"Any other ships around?" Hawking asks, breaking the silence.

"No, sir." Jasmine answers. "They just seem to be off on some kind of joy ride."

"Tactical, extend range with your targeting sensors." Atany says. "I want you to check behind us."

"Idea?" Hawking asks.

"Hunch." Atany answers. Fifteen seconds pass.

"They're slowing down even more." Jasmine informs the crew.

"Captain, your hunch was correct." Lieutenant Commander Sacar says. "There are two more fluctuations coming in behind us. We'll be in their sensor range in two point five minutes."

"We've been baited." Atany says, alarmed but calm.

"They just don't know they have us yet." Hawking adds.

"Oh yeah. Fuck you." Atany begins. "Helm, full impulse for thirty seconds. Tactical, as soon as you can, take out the two fluctuations in front of us." She activates her intercom. "Daniel, do you have a plan yet?"

"Yes, just need to know how many targets?" He answers.

"Two targets. Get your collective asses to the transporter room and stand by." She deactivates the unit.

"Tactical, fire at will." She says.

"Yes, captain." Sacar responds and complies.

"Helm, when those two ships are toast, get us within transporter range of the ships behind us but keep us out of their sensor range."

"Will do, captain."

"Firing." Comes from tactical. The energy bolts appear on the screen and race toward their targets. Three seconds pass and impact explosions can be seen. When the flash subsides two Horatha cruisers hang motionless in the vacuum of space.

"Fire again." Atany orders.

"Firing." Sacar says as he does. The bolts of energy scream towards the disabled ships. In seconds the defenseless ships are vaporized by the Forzak weapons.

"Helm, engage." Atany commands.

"Engaging." Levi repeats and the stars on the screen sharply shift to the right, indicating a port side banking maneuver. The battleship finishes it's turn and heads towards the two fluctuations now in front of them.

"Sacar, fire as they come to bear."

"Got it, captain." The energy bolts appear on the screen and explode, exposing the two other Horatha cruisers." Atany hits her intercom.

Transporter room, beam them over now." The captain's voice stern.

"Transport complete." Comes from the intercom. Silence fills the air. Twenty minutes pass and all is quiet. The two ships on the screen continue to hang motionless.

Captain, a transporter beam has just completed its cycle and seven items are in the hanger deck by the Deliverance." Jasmine informs the captain. Before Atany can respond, the ship on the left explodes in a brilliant flash.

"What the fuck just happened?" Atany yells at Jasmine in excitement. She hits her intercom again.

"Transporter room, are our people back?" Nervousness is in her voice.

"Not yet, captain." Is the response.

"Jasmine, scan the other ship. See if our people are there."

"On it." After a few seconds, "Found seven life signs that are not Horatha." Jasmine reports. "I don't know how they did it but they made it to the other ship."

"That's why they're the archangels." Atany explains. She relaxes a bit. Everyone on the bridge is staring at the ship on the screen, wondering how their shipmates are doing. Twenty minutes go by without any sign.

The Horatha ship explodes in a flash equally as brilliant as the first one. The sudden explosion catches everyone off guard. Once the crew regain their composure Jasmine spins and scans the area.

"All seven personnel near the Deliverance, with more mechanical components." Jasmine reports. Atany releases a deep sigh of relief. She stands and heads toward the turbolift.

"Levi, you have the bridge. I'll be in the hanger deck. Roeton, have Benjamin meet me there." The door closes.

The captain enters the hanger deck and, before the door closes, Benjamin enters quickly. The archangels are standing in a tight group, sorting the electronic components on the floor. The two join them.

"Welcome back." Atany says and gives her husband a respectable kiss in front of her crew. "What's this stuff?"

"Three invisibility shield generators and twelve emitter arrays." Daniel answers with a sly, contagious smile.

"Cool." She replies with a huge grin. "How did everything go?"

"As smooth as Brantaxian silk." He tells her. She looks at Benjamin, who is kneeling, inspecting the components.

"How's it looking, Benjamin?" She asks him.

"There won't be any problem integrating the components into the current matrix but I can't guarantee the generator technology will be compatible with Forzak energy frequencies."

"Let's take it one step at a time." Atany suggests with strong intent. "Get these components installed without making the primary power connection. We'll deal with the power problem at that time."

"Okay then, captain. I'll get a couple of my techs up here and get this stuff installed." Benjamin agrees. "We'll have to do several space-walks to secure the emitters so you'll have to stop the ship for a time."

"Just let me know when we need to stop." She tells him.

"I'll call the bridge when we're ready." He finishes.

"Great. Make it happen." She tells him as he stands and goes to the intercom on the wall. He contacts the drive section and orders all non-essential personnel to assist. They acknowledge.

The captain and the archangels leave the hanger deck to debrief and relax. Seconds later the two Rillians along with Lieutenants Diana and Aurora enter the hanger deck. Thirty seconds later Lieutenant Borkin, pilot and cook enters with nurses Nazay and Ephasiah.

Forty-five minutes pass and the bridge is quiet. The ship is on course for the planetoid that houses their basecamp. The sensors show the area clear of any other vessels. The captain and first officer are at their posts.

● ● ●

Hawking and Daniel are at their stations. Lieutenants Torres and Hoon are at respective stations. Everyone is waiting for Benjamin and his team to accomplish their assignment.

"Captain, Benjamin is signaling." Roeton tells her.

"On speaker." She tells him. He acknowledges.

"Go ahead, Benjamin." She says.

"Captain, we are ready for the spacewalk." Benjamin reports. "I have two teams working in sync. I can't say how long but we'll get done as quick as we can."

"Understood. Proceed in fifteen seconds." She replies.

"Acknowledged." The line goes dead.

"Levi, all stop."

"All stop, aye."

The ship quickly slows to a stop. Once stopped, she is allowed to drift while the team does their job.

"Aurora, Diana, are you two in place" Benjamin asks from a station on the bridge, by Professor Hawking.

"Aurora here, I'm ready."

"Diana here, I'm in place."

"Borkin, beam the teams in place." Benjamin tells him and he slides the controls. On the platform, Nazay, one of the Tartarus' nurses, and Katra'el, one of the Rillian defectors, dressed in spacesuits and holding a shield emitter, fade away in the blue sparkles and spiraling, silvery glitter of the Forzak transporter beam.

When the transport cycle finishes, Ephasiah, the other of the Tartarus' two nurses, and the second Rillian defector, S'squaad, carrying a shield emitter, step onto the platform and are beamed to their location.

The first team materializes at the nose of the huge ship, about two meters off the hull. They float to an outside access hatch for the navigational deflector array. Using handheld gamma welders, they melt the emitter to the hull plating above the access hatch.

• • •

"Emitter array in place." Nazay says into her communicator after about twenty minutes. "It's on you now, Diana."

"I'm working on it." Diana says as she uses a gamma welder to cut through the hull behind the array.

"Our emitter is in place. Go ahead, Aurora." Ephasiah says minutes after Nazay announced their completion. Ephasiah and S'squaad placed their unit on the rear of the ship, in between and above the engine ports.

"This one is hooked up." Diana announces after fifteen minutes. In that time she was able to cut a piece of hull plating behind the array out and wire the emitter to an exposed E.P.S. conduit.

"This one's done." Aurora says a few minutes after Diana.

"Good job everyone." Benjamin says. "Borkin, transport everyone to their second locations."

"Transport cycle complete. Everyone is where they need to be." Borkin answers after a minute. It takes six and three quarter hours to complete the project. All twelve emitter arrays are used. Apart from the ones on the front and back, one is placed on the bottom and the top of the drive section. One is just behind the hanger deck doors as well as the top of the center section, between the two antennae arrays. One is put under the nose section as well as one above the bridge. There are also two attached to each of the two weapons arrays, one fore and one aft.

While the two teams are out on their spacewalks, Lieutenant Commander Merari, engineer's mate is with Lieutenant Commander Reuben, communications officer on B shift, in the drive section connecting E.P.S. conduits, attached to the emitter arrays, to the invisibility shield generators. Once the conduits are hard wired to the generators, the two need to reroute power, via the computer, to power the arrays and show that everything is connected properly. When they are sure the conduits are connected and operational, Merari contacts the bridge.

"Merari to the bridge." He says into his intercom console.

"What's up, Merari?" Atany asks.

"All the power conduits are attached to the shield generators and functioning properly, captain." He tells her as Lieutenant Commander Benjamin comes into his view.

"Very good, Merari." Atany says. "The others are finished outside and Benjamin should be joining you any time."

"He just walked in, captain." Merari answers.

"Good." She replies. "We'll be on our way down momentarily."

Five minutes later the drive section doors open. Atany and Daniel enter the room, followed by Fental and Hawking. The six converge on a table placed by one of the five turbine generators used to power the electrical needs of the ship. On the table are the three invisibility shield generators connected to a series of thick wires used to power the emitter arrays.

"Supplemental power input indicates all the equipment will operate properly, captain." Merari says when they gather.

"How do we get power from there to there?" Atany asks as she motions her hand from the turbine to the generator. Everyone contemplates.

"The same way we did it on the Heaven." Hawking says.

"Explain." Atany orders.

"The universal plasma phase converter." He reminds the group. "Using it in reverse should allow us to input Forzak energy and get power suitable for the Horatha generators."

"We can use the one installed in the Deliverance." Fental suggests.

"Did anyone happen to find a spare one on this ship?" Daniel asks. "If we damage the one on the Deliverance, we won't be able to replace it. It was made for that system. If we find one designed for this ship, it will handle the power output."

"That's a good point, captain." Benjamin adds.

"That is a good point." Fental agrees. "Sorry."

"Sorry?" Atany says more than asks. "Don't be sorry. It's a good idea. Try to find one designed for this ship. They didn't need it but maybe they have a spare for this ship, or at least the parts to build one."

"Daniel, Hawking, you're with me. We'll check the starboard half. You three check the port half. With luck we'll find it soon." The group breaks up into two teams and head off to find a universal plasma phase converter somewhere in the recesses of this huge ship.

CHAPTER 4

"Captain's log, stardate 30246.09. With the genius of Professor Hawking and Lieutenant Commander Benjamin and the components found throughout the drive section, we've constructed a duplicate plasma phase converter. It has been installed and needs only to be powered up."

"Are you guys all set down there?" Atany asks into her intercom.

"We'll be set in one minute." Hawking's voice sounds. "We need to lock down the interface more securely then we'll be ready."

"Alright, let me know when you've got everything ready." She says and deactivates the intercom.

"Levi, how long before we reach our planetoid if we go to warp two?" The captain asks.

"We'll arrive in three point two hours." He answers her.

"Good. Do it now." She says. The ship starts to move slowly for several seconds then, in the blink of an eye, it accelerates to seven million, three hundred and eighty thousand kilometers per second.

"We're ready, captain." Hawking's voice comes through Atany's intercom in the time he stated earlier.

"Activate a level four force field around the area you're working then power up the plasma converter." She tells him.

"Will do." He answers.

"Daniel, can you get the section of the engine room they're in on the screen?" Atany asks her husband.

"I think I can." He answers. "Give me a minute to configure the internal sensors." He starts manipulating controls and adjusting dials and the main viewscreen starts to flicker. Within seconds the flickering screen shows the inside of the drive section.

Daniel adjusts several more controls and the image zooms in on the table where the two men are working. Hawking is scanning the components with a tricorder while Benjamin is tapping on a pad. In a flash a blue, hazy, force field, from ceiling to floor, surrounds the table along with the men.

"Activate the unit, professor." Atany says from her seat, watching on the bridge. Hawking turns the converter on. The lights on the unit glow brightly, indicating power is flowing through it's circuits.

"Congratulations, gentlemen." Atany says to them. "You're still alive and my ship is still intact."

"No one is happier about that than us, captain." Benjamin comments.

"Are you ready to activate the generators?" Atany continues.

"Ready as we'll ever be." Hawking says as he activates the three units. Translucent panels around each of the generators begin to glow dully, pulsing slowly. The dull, pulsing glow steadily brightens as the pulsing speeds up. Within seconds the panels are glowing steady and strong.

• • •

"Congratulations again." Atany says.

"Captain," Fental interrupts, "how do we know the generators are actually making the ship invisible?" Atany thinks about Fental's question for several seconds. She lowers her head, resting her forehead in her hand. She slowly rocks her head side to side.

"Professor, shut everything down." Atany says loudly.

"What's wrong captain?" He asks with confusion on his face as he shuts the two components down.

"I'll ask you what I was just asked." She answers. "How do we know the generators are actually working properly?" The two men on the screen look somewhat perplexed.

"Fuck!" Hawking shouts loudly as he face palms himself in the forehead with a meaty slap sound, clearly heard by everyone on the bridge.

"Levi, bring us to a stop. Jasmine, get in your XV and set yourself five hundred meters off the port bow."

"Yes, ma'am." Levi says as he adjusts the controls.

"On my way." Jasmine says as she gets up from the auxiliary science station and heads for the turbolift. Sixteen minutes later a message comes in on an open frequency. Roeton puts it on speaker.

"I'm in position, captain." Jasmine's voice comes through clearly. "I've got a clear view of the ship."

"Hawking, power up the converter." She says and she watches as he does. He powers up the generators again and, again, the lights pulse to life like before.

Jasmine, sitting in her cockpit five hundred meters off the port bow, sees the massive battleship slowly fade away, becoming completely invisible. Her eyes widen as her jaw hangs open. She sits, mesmerized for a few seconds.

"Captain, it works perfectly." She says excitedly.

"Very cool." The captain's voice sounds through the small ship's communications panel. Several seconds pass.

"Now for the hard part." Atany says.

"What do you mean 'hard part'?" Jasmine asks with the sound of concern in her voice.

"Lieutenant, we need to test the shield generators while we are under flight. You are going to follow alongside and let me know if there are any fluctuations in the shields." Atany explains.

"How, pray tell, can I do that? I can't see you and my instruments don't show you."

"Levi, give Jasmine the course setting to run parallel to us."

"Jasmine," Levi says, "set course two, two, one mark zero, zero, three."

"Course set." She replies to her shipmates.

"Levi, one quarter impulse." Atany orders and he complies.

"Jasmine, go to full thrusters." Levi says as the Tartarus starts to move.

"Going full burn." She says as she slides the control handle in her left hand forward. The little ship quickly speeds along, adjusting its course automatically.

"Captain, we can go to three quarter impulse if I tell Lieutenant Jasmine when to hit her turbo." Levi informs Atany.

"Even better." Atany says. "Do it."

"Aye, captain, going to three quarter impulse." He makes the necessary adjustments and the ship speeds up. They continue on course for thirty minutes, no issues being reported from any department.

"Jasmine, kick in your turbo thruster for thirty seconds." Levi tells the lone pilot.

"Copy that." She responds as she pushes the left button on her control stick, holding it down. The turbo thruster kicks in and the ship nearly triples in speed. Thirty seconds go by and she releases the button and the ship returns to its original speed.

"That is one fast little ship." Levi says aloud with admiration for the technological advancement demonstrated in the vessel.

"Just how fast is that thing?" Fental asks.

"We're reading eighty-six thousand, five hundred kilometers a second, just over three quarter impulse." He answers.

"Holy shit, that's fast." Atany says, impressed.

"Especially in a single seat ship." Fental adds, making Atany think.

"Hit your turbo thruster again for thirty seconds." Levi tells Jasmine.

"Copy." She says and does.

"Where is she?" Atany asks Levi.

"Five thousand kilometers ahead and a bit to port." He answers.

"Good. Increase speed to full impulse. Make sure Jasmine keeps up." The captain orders. Fifteen minutes pass.

"Jasmine," Levi's voice comes through her communications panel again after only fifteen minutes.

"Go ahead." She replies to the disembodied voice.

"Hit your turbo thruster for forty-five seconds." He tells her.

"Hitting turbo thruster." She says as she complies. Twenty-five minutes pass. An image appearing on the right side of Jasmine's fighter catches her eye. A massive distortion affect becomes more visible and, after a number of seconds, the Tartarus becomes visible.

"Jasmine to Tartarus." The lone pilot says into her microphone.

"What's up, Lieutenant?" Atany asks.

"Captain, the ship is visible again." She informs her commander.

"Good." Atany responds. "Get back in here.

"Roger that." Jasmine answers. Through her cockpit canopy she sees the ship slow to a near stop.

She pulls a tight circle, coming in from behind and under the huge ship. She sees the outer doors open and inches her way into the small compartment. Once the outer door close, the inner door opens. Jasmine brings her ship straight up into the upper compartment, landing only when the inner door closes. She exits her ship when the room fully pressurizes. She exits the room, heading for the bridge.

Jasmine steps onto the bridge and takes her seat at the auxiliary science station.

"Good job, Jasmine." Atany tells her with a smile and a 'thumbs up'.

"Thanks, captain." She replies with a smile.

"Levi, warp five. Get us to base."

"E.T.A. one point seven hours." Levi says.

The ship glides into orbit around the planetoid that houses the base for the ex-Alliance crew. The captain looks around the bridge.

"Roeton, have Lieutenant Commander Rigel come to the bridge then let the crew know that I will be granting shore leave in two eighteen hour shifts starting at the end of this duty rotation." Atany orders.

"Daniel." She says. When he looks at her, she shifts her head in a manner indicating she wants him to come over. He picks up on her signal and walks over to her, standing very near Fental.

"Professor." She shouts in the other direction, motioning him the same way as she did Daniel. He comes over, standing in front of her.

"When Jasmine was out there during our test, I sat here wondering what it would be like." She says to Daniel, Hawking and Fental.

"What would what be like?" Daniel asks.

"Flying those XV's." Atany says with her usual, huge smile.

"Are you serious?" Daniel asks her.

"Of course." She answers. "We're all experienced shuttle pilots. Why not get a little fly time in those ships?"

"Count me in." Hawking says. "I've thought about those ships too."

"Me too." Fental says.

* * *

"I'm in." Daniel adds.

"Good. Lieutenant Commander Rigel should be here any second." Atany tells them.

"You asked for me, captain?" Rigel says when Atany finishes, startling the four huddled together.

"Speak of the devil and you get a Rigel." Atany smiles bright and wide at the young pilot.

"Yes, Rigel." The captain continues after several seconds. "I want you to teach the four of us the finer points of flying your XV's."

"Excuse me, captain?" Rigel asks in near disbelief.

"We are all experienced shuttle pilots so give us a rundown on the controls and how to operate the different systems."

"With all due respect to everyone here," Rigel says with a serious tone. "The XV is nothing like a shuttle."

"We are aware." Atany says politely. "Teach us the basics and we'll take them away from the gravitational pull of the planetoid to practice our skills."

"I'll agree to this." Rigel says. "You learn the operational protocols to my satisfaction then you can take them out."

"Agreed." Atany says and the other three follow suit.

"When do you want to start?" Rigel asks.

"No better time than right now." Atany says.

"Where do you want to do this?" Rigel continues.

"In the briefing room down the hall will work." Atany says and the five make their way down the hall.

They enter the briefing room and sit around the table in the middle of the room. Hawking's face is buried in a pad while his fingers work the controls at a feverish pitch.

Rigel looks at the four officers, nervousness showing through her attempt at a calm demeanor. She stands.

"You'll have to excuse me," She starts with a quivering voice, "I've never taught a class before."

* * *

"Give me a couple of minutes and I'll have something to help us all." Hawking says as he looks up from the pad. He sees the acknowledgements of his shipmates and buries himself back into his work.

Hawking finishes in just over two minutes. He ends his programming with a huge, long yawn.

"Sorry." He says. "Here you go, Lieutenant Commander." He says to Rigel as he hands her the pad.

"Thank you." She says as she takes it. She activates the pad and the viewscreen on the wall behind her flickers to life.

The display on the half-wall size viewscreen is a simplified diagram of the three walls of the XV's cockpit, showing all the operational controls. Each control marked by a number with the control identifications listed along the right side of the screen.

"This image is the XV cockpit." Rigel says. "How did you get this? All this data is classified and encrypted."

"I designed a lot of the software on that ship." Hawking explains. "Nothing is classified to me."

"I thought you're an archeologist." She comments.

"I am." He responds with a smile.

"Multitalented?" She half-asks, curiosity in her voice.

"Yes, yes I am." He answers. Atany giggles and nods in agreement as her eyes lock with the professors.

"These fighters, unlike the shuttles you're used to flying, are capable of near light speed. They incorporate a micro inertial dampener. The pilot feels none of the gee forces that would otherwise splatter our bodies into the seats. That would be very messy." Rigel begins. She gets everyone to smile and eases up when she sees it.

"The sensitivity of the controls is another issue that will be of concern. You must practice slowly at first."

"What's the concern?" Daniel asks.

"Because there are no gee forces, the pilot has to watch the controls when within any gravitational field because the ship does

have stress tolerances and if you aren't careful the ship will disinte-
grate."

"I see." He responds.

"Before you can even get in the cockpit, you have to know
the control systems. On the screen is the cockpit from the seated
position. We'll start with the forward controls."

Rigel spends the next two hours explaining every control and
operational protocol needed to safely fly the XV. She quizzes them
until she is satisfied that they know all the technical aspects of the
ship.

"Well, captain, that's all I can teach you." Rigel tells Atany.
"It's up to the four of you to get out there and practice. I'll follow in
the Deliverance and someone will have to keep a transporter lock on
all of you."

"Atany to bridge." She says after she activates the intercom
panel. "How long before crew rotation?" She asks.

"Three point five hours." Levi's disembodied voice answers.

"Thank you. Out." She replies and hits the intercom button
twice.

"Engineering." She says into the device.

"Benjamin here, captain."

"Commander, I need all four XV's and the Deliverance
fueled and prepped for flight in three hours."

"Will do, captain."

"I also need someone assigned to the transporter room for a
shift approximately four hours long to begin when the five ships depart."

"I'll get it done."

"I know you will. Out." She deactivates the intercom. "Well,
we have three hours. I suggest we use that time to become familiar
with the cockpits and the controls." She stands, as do the other four,
and they head out the door.

"You did good as a teacher." Hawking tells Rigel.

"Thanks. I was nervous as a fuck."

"Well, you didn't show it." Fental adds.

"Thanks. I appreciate it." She replies as they head to the hanger deck.

Three point five hours pass and the bridge crew rotation comes on duty. The current duty cycle head off to their quarters then to the surface for fresh air, green grass and sunshine.

In the hanger deck, the four would-be pilots sit in the fighters with Rigel at the controls of the Deliverance. They wait patiently until the duty rotation change is over. It takes another five minutes.

"Atany to bridge. Merah, bring the ship one million kilometers away from the planet." Atany says from the cockpit of XV1. "Inform me when we get there." She switches a dial on the communications panel.

"Transporter room, maintain a constant lock on Fental, Hawking, Daniel and myself. Do not let the locks break. Emergency beam out coordinates are on the Deliverance.

"Will do, captain." Aurora's voice comes through the radio. "Locks are set and ready."

"Outstanding." Atany says excitedly.

There are several seconds of silence. The radio beeps.

"Bridge to Atany. We are one million kilometers from the planet."

"All stop. Maintain position. We are taking the XV's out for training maneuvers. Keep long range scanners active."

"Aye, captain."

The hanger deck doors open and the five ships drop slowly from the belly of the massive battleship. They drift apart, giving a wide berth for each of the pilot trainees. All five ships simultaneously move forward, accelerating at uneven rates, making the formation look sloppy.

It takes several kilometers before they are back in proper formation. It takes several more kilometers for the four to be able to fly in unison. The four, again in unison, hit their turbos and speed off

· · ·

ahead of the Deliverance, which increases speed a second later. After about thirty seconds they shut their turbos down and continue at combat speed, followed closely by Rigel.

They spend the next three hours learning basic maneuvering, spread far apart. They spent the next hour practicing flying in loose formation. Four and a half hours pass when they call it quits for the day. One at a time they slowly bring the fighters into the hanger deck, both doors allowed to open fully before anyone tries to land.

After the five ships are in place the doors close and the bay repressurizes. The five crewmates gather together at the hangerbay entry doors.

"That was amazing!" Fental shouts. A smile spreads across her face.

"Exhilarating!" Daniel says.

"I can't wait to do it again." Hawking says enthusiastically.

"I'm with Hawking." Atany says. "But there's time for that later. For now we've got to get to the bridge." The four head to the turbolift at the end of the long hall.

The Tartarus glides back into orbit around the tiny planetoid that the crew now calls home. Rather than go to the surface, the four would-be fighter pilots return to their quarters and all fall into deep sleeps.

Eleven hours pass and the crew rotation begins. The bridge crew is newly in place when Atany and Daniel come off of the turbolift. They take their perspective positions. The captain looks over the end of duty reports and signs off on them. All systems check out normally as the rotation begins.

Eighteen hours pass and the crewmen on the surface have returned and are now reporting for duty. The crew rotation is complete. The captain orders the duty rotation to return to twelve hours.

Atany sits in her command seat, lost in thought, staring at the star pattern on the main viewscreen. Fental sits in her seat beside the captain, wondering what's running through her head.

"What's up, captain?" Dutona finally asks softly.

"I'm just thinking about what to do next." She confides in her first officer. "We have this ship, with all these bells and whistles, and now I think it's time to recruit new members and bring peace to the quadrant."

"Where do we start?" She asks her boss, a look of inquisitiveness comes across her face.

"We're going to the research station." She answers.

"Why there?" She looks puzzled.

"Professors Arad Zor and Servik Brickman." Atany answers.

"Zor the astrophysicist and Brickman the theoretical physicist? Why them?" The look of puzzlement is more prevalent.

"We need more people who can help figure out the systems on this ship. If something breaks down I'd like to have more than two capable minds working on the problem. Remember, this ship is a thousand years old."

"I see your point." Fental responds.

"Who knows," Atany continues, "we may find a few more able hands to join our cause."

"What cause is that, captain?" Fental now showing concern.

"Total peace by complete domination, of course." Atany answers matter-of-factly. Disbelief sweeps across Fental's face. An eerie silence fills the room for several seconds.

"Helm," Atany says, "set a course for the research station. Warp six."

"Aye, ma'am. E.T.A. five hours." Levi answers, unaware of the captain's last remark.

"After we pick up Zor and Brickman," Atany says to Fental, softly after leaning in close to her so no one else hears, "I think we'll go to Brantax Three and get Professor Hawking's associates."

"Why?" Fental asks. "Why would you want to do that?"

● ● ●

"Now that we've found the Forzak homeworld, and this ship, I'm wondering what else the Forzak have left behind. With the help of the professor's associates, we're going to find out."

"What if they don't want to help you?"

"Ah, Fental." Atany says with a smile and nonchalant demeanor. "How can anyone say no to us, especially since we have this ship? Really, with these guns pointed at you, would you say no?" She slowly turns her head and stares blankly at the viewscreen. Fental sits back quietly, her face showing the fear that her mind is generating as she envisions what the captain has just told her.

"There is one more thing I need to do to solidify this union and I need you to bear witness." Atany tells Fental after a few minutes. She stands and Fental follows suit.

"Professor, Daniel, will you two follow us, please?" Atany asks.

The two men follow the two women down the hall and into the conference room. Atany stands at the head of the conference table as the other three sit close.

"As we start to build our crew I find I myself remiss for waiting so long to do this." The three look up at her slightly confused.

"Of the twenty-seven crewmembers on this ship, only one is not an Alliance officer and I'd like to rectify that now. Professor, would you come here?" She politely orders and Hawking complies.

"Professor Aristotle Hawking." Atany says with a polite smile. "By the powers vested in me as captain of this vessel, for your invaluable service to this ship and crew in the successful conclusion of our mission, I proudly bestow onto you, the rank of commander, in service of this vessel." Her smile widens and she gives him a solid kiss.

"Thank you, captain." Hawking says to her. "I don't know what to say about this."

"Don't say anything. Go put your new uniform on and come back to the bridge and man your station."

"Just one question before I go." He says.

* * *

"What's that, commander?"

"Where exactly do I get my new uniform?"

"Oh yeah, sorry." She says. "Go to the Deliverance and use the replicator there."

"Computer," Atany says aloud, "record in the log, as of this stardate, the commission of Aristotle Hawking to the rank of commander and assigned to the Tartarus."

Daniel and Fental stand and congratulate Hawking. The four leave the room. Hawking goes toward the hanger deck as the other three head for the bridge.

Commander Hawking steps onto the bridge about forty-five minutes after Atany, Daniel and Fental. Everyone turns when the door opens and they all do a double-take when they see Hawking in an Alliance uniform.

He takes his position at his science station, analyzing the data coming from the sensor array. After a handful of seconds he lifts his head away from the monitor and looks around the room.

"Thank you." He says with a smile, waving is hand. "Thank you, everyone." Everyone smiles and return to their duties.

CHAPTER 5

"Captain's log, stardate 30301.41. We are fifteen minutes away from Research Station Alpha. Once Professor's Zor and Brickman are on board, we will liberate anyone who wishes to join me then move on to Brantax Three for Hawking's associates."

"Slow to full impulse." Atany says to Levi.

"Slowing to full impulse power." He repeats as he complies. The streaking star pattern on the screen suddenly becomes static as the ship drops out of warp speed. A few seconds pass and the station becomes visible on the screen. Starting as a small dot, it quickly becomes larger.

Research Station Alpha is the last of a series of such stations built during the second age of discovery, when civilizations throughout the quadrant began to discover space flight… and each other.

The station is made up of two one thousand meter diameter saucers. Each saucer is five decks high and contains six docking ports, located on deck three and evenly spaced. There are six fin-like protrusions in the shape of triangles attached on one side of the saucer. These triangles are thirty degrees by sixty degrees by ninety degrees.

The fins are taller on the outer edge, being seven decks tall, and angle down towards the center, down to two decks at the center, where the six converge. These sections are located between the docking ports all the way around, with the look of spokes when seen from the top. Each fin contains a wide range of laboratories, capable of duplicating any condition found throughout the quadrant.

The two saucers are connected by a one thousand meter long, five deck tall corridor measuring fifteen meters wide. The middle five hundred meters measure ten meters wider on two sides. The third side extends two decks and the fourth side extends four decks. Mounted on top of these decks is the communications array. On the two evenly extended sides are mounted framing for the large solar sails, used to collect light from the surrounding stars to power parts of the station.

"Roeton, open hailing frequencies." She orders.

"Hailing frequencies open." He replies.

"This is Captain Dinema Atany of the Allia… of the starship Tartarus calling Research Station Alpha. Come in, please." Her voice pleasant sounding and her smile wide and bright.

"This is Research Station Alpha." A pleasant female voice sounds through the intercom system. "How may we be of assistance?"

"We would like permission to come aboard and speak with Professors Arad Zor and Servik Brickman." Atany answers. There is a brief silence.

"They are in the starboard laboratory hub, section delta nine." The voice informs them. "Authorization to board is granted. Have a good day."

"You as well," Atany says, "and good health." She stands and looks around the bridge.

* * *

"I am going alone. I'll be back in thirty minutes." Atany tells her crew as she heads to the turbolift.

The captain enters the transporter room to find Lieutenant Cylar Voltarus at the controls.

"Thank you for coming, Lieutenant." Atany says with a smile. "You understand what I need you to do, right?"

"Crystal clear, Captain. Just give the word." He responds.

"Excellent." She says as she steps onto the transporter platform.

"Energize." She says to the young archangel. She fades away in blue, sparkling, spirals of light and sound.

"Daniel, do you have a minute?" Fental says to the captain's husband. He turns to her and sees the look of concern on her face.

"What's going on?" He asks.

"Not here." She replies as she looks around. "Come with me."

He gets up and the two leave the bridge via the hall and head toward the conference room. Once inside she turns to him.

"Do you have any idea what Dinema has in mind?" The sound of cautious concern emanating from her lips.

"Of course I do." He tells her nonchalantly.

"And you're okay with this?" She asks with growing concern.

"Why wouldn't I be?" His expression plainly showing a genuine lack of understanding as to why Fental is questioning the captain.

"Because she wants to take over the quadrant and rule it herself." She replies with an increasing tone of seriousness.

"And, you've got to admit, with this ship she, we, can do it." He tells her in the same matter-of-factly tone that Dinema used. The one that started her mind racing with concern.

"Let's face it, Fental," He smiles widely at her, "we've got the ship. With a handful more crew we can defeat any and all enemies that rise up and try to overthrow us."

"How long have the two of you been planning this?"

"I thought about it the minute I saw this thing. I found out later that she thought about it at the same time. Are you going to stand there and tell me that you never thought about it?"

"Of course I did."

"Then why fight it?" He looks slightly more serious. "**We** are here now. **We** have this ship. **We** are in control. What do you think the Alliance will do with this?"

"This isn't what we signed up for." She starts.

"Don't be naive, Dutona." Daniel cuts in more sympathetically. "Some hot shot admiral is gonna see this ship, put two and two together and we'll be the one's having to fight against this monster." He pauses for a second. "What team do you want to be on, Dutona, the masters or the servants?"

"I want to be on the team that isn't corrupted by power and violence."

"You might want to consider joining the team that will, ultimately, cause less destruction with less violence. That's right where you are now, Fental." He gently puts his hands on her shoulders for comfort.

"Where do you draw the line when it comes to too violent?" She asks him with compassion in her voice and her eyes reflecting the same.

"How about this?" He asks. "You and I will keep an eye on Dinema. If she gets out of control we can be her conscience."

"Okay, that'll work." Relief screaming from her words.

Daniel gives Dutona a kiss, softly at first. Within seconds his kiss becomes more sensual, his tongue gently parting her lips. She parts her lips wider, inviting his tongue into her mouth. Fental's head starts to spin in ecstasy and excitement.

The two separate after a few minutes. The look of enjoyment shows on both of their faces. It takes several seconds for the two to regain their composure.

"Shall we go back to the bridge?" He asks half out of breath.

"Not yet." She answers as she pushes him back against the conference table. His back hits the table with a dull thud.

She squats down in front of him. She grabs his uniform slacks and pulls them down quickly, pulling each of his legs out of the clothing. When she finishes, she starts to stand slowly, sliding her hands gently on the outside of his legs. As she approaches his hips, her path is blocked by his large, erect penis. She examines his hard on and eagerly slides it into her mouth, moaning as she takes it all the way in.

Daniel begins to moan uncontrollably as she slides his cock in and out of her mouth. On the fifth thrust he stops her and pulls her up to her feet. He spins around, leaning her against the table. Daniel returns the favor by sliding Fental's slacks off.

After removing the slacks from Fental's body, Daniel starts to stand. He stops at the top of her thighs and, feeling the heat emanating from between her legs, darts his face straight into her pussy. He runs his tongue over her swollen clit and she starts to moan deeply. After several minutes he stands and grabs Fental's right leg, spreading her open, as he stands facing her, their eyes locking.

Without saying a word or breaking eye contact, Daniel flexes his cock, positioning the head at the entrance of Dutona's soaked pussy. He leans in, locking his lips onto Fental's. As her tongue slams against his, he thrusts his rock hard cock deep inside her.

Fental's moans grow louder with each of Daniel's deeply penetrating thrusts. By the third thrust Daniel starts to moan uncontrollably as Fental's pussy grips tightly to his throbbing shaft.

Daniel's thrusts are slow, long and deliberate, each stroke intensifying the feeling for them both. Fifteen minutes pass. As Fental's body starts to spasm into its third orgasm, Daniel starts to feel the approach of his orgasm. Three strokes later they simultaneously orgasm, holding each other tightly as their legs weaken and they fall clumsily to the floor, neither wanting their bodies to separate.

It takes a solid five minutes before either could speak.

"That was awesome." Fental says in between spurts of heavy breathing. "But we've got to get back to work." She stands with effort and gathers her cloths. As she dresses, Daniel collects his clothes and starts dressing.

"We should do that again when we have more time." Daniel says with his sly smile of charm.

"Any time." She smiles back. They finish dressing and leave the room.

"Can I ask you something personal?" Fental asks Daniel.

"You can ask me anything you'd like." He answers.

"How is it you and Atany can be married yet have casual sex with other people? Doesn't that make your marriage complicated?"

"It's simple." Daniel begins. "I know Dinema loves me, of that there is no doubt. In our journeys we meet a vast amount of people and, you'll agree, there are just some people you can't help being attracted to."

"Yes, but being married, shouldn't you fight those urges?"

"Why waste the energy fighting it? Get it out of your system and let the friendship grow and strengthen. I know Dinema won't leave me and she knows I won't ever leave her. I also know that because of their relationship, Hawking won't ever hurt her or allow her to be hurt. I know she's safe. Because of our relationship, you should know that I will never hurt you or allow you to be hurt."

"What happens if either of you become smitten with someone who is married?" Fental asks with genuine curiosity.

"As long as they are like-minded there is no problem." He answers.

"What do you mean, 'Like-minded'?"

"If Atany takes to someone who's married, she can only have him if his wife is willing to be with me, and vice versa, if I'm taken by someone, she knows that as long as Atany gets her husband, we can indulge. No guilt, no anger. Our love for each other, being as strong as it is, allows us to enjoy these freedoms. It makes life so much more pleasurable. And it's not like it happens often."

"I love that philosophy." Dutona says with a huge smile as the two enter the bridge.

"I'll see you after shift." She tells him as he heads to the science station and she takes her seat.

"Looking forward to it already." He says as he continues to his station.

Atany materializes in the center of a large lab. There are two dozen, at least, scientists working and bickering and arguing subjects well beyond the captain's understanding.

She approaches a small group and taps one of them on the shoulder.

"Professor Zor?" She asks politely. The young woman points to three people at a computer console at the far end of the room.

"Thank you." Atany responds.

"You're welcome." The woman responds with a voice so deep it makes Atany's stomach vibrate. She turns and walks toward the trio.

"Excuse me." Atany says as she approaches the three. "Which one of you is Professor Zor?"

"I am Professor Zor." Comes from the moderately attractive, middle-aged, redhead in the center.

"I need to speak with you and Professor Brickman concerning an issue of great importance and sensitivity."

"Well, it's your lucky day. I'm Professor Brickman."

"Excellent!" The captain says with subdued excitement. "I am Captain Dinema Atany of the starship Tartarus."

"How may we be of assistance?"

"As I said, it is of a sensitive nature."

* * *

Hearing this, the third of the trio leaves to tend to other matters.

"Are you familiar with the legend of the Forzak Empire?"

"Yes!" Zor says with surprise and astonishment. "We all are."

"Then you are aware of the Alliance mission to locate the Forzak homeworld?"

"We've heard rumors mostly." Zor continues. "Nothing substantiated."

"I am the captain of that mission." Atany tells them. "I am here to offer the two of you the opportunity of a lifetime." Their attention is captured. Atany pauses for dramatic effect.

"I am currently in command of the starship Tartarus. It is a one thousand year old Forzak battleship."

"And it's still operational?" Brickman asks in disbelief.

"Fully." Atany replies.

"Amazing." Zor answers with equal astonishment. "I have a million questions. I don't know where to start, so I'll start with the most obvious,

What is your offer?"

"I'm glad you started with that one." Dinema confesses. "The two of you are uniquely qualified to assist me and my crew. We need your expertise on our ship to help unlock its secrets." Both scientists are too stunned to speak right away. Several seconds pass. The two discuss the issue quietly.

"Can you give us an hour to wrap things up here?" Zor asks.

"Of course." Atany says slightly surprised. "I honestly thought it would take much more convincing to get you to join me."

"Well, like you said," Brickman answers, "It's an opportunity of a lifetime and our work here isn't nearly as important or fascinating as what you're offering."

"Awesome. Contact my ship when you're ready. In the meantime I will make sure your quarters are ready when you get there."

"Very good." Zor replies. "We'll see you in about an hour."

"See you then." Atany responds. She walks away from the two as a huge smile spreads across her face. She takes her communicator.

"Atany here. Beam me up." She sparkles into nothingness.

The captain exits the turbolift on the bridge of her ship and takes her seat.

"How did the recruitment drive go?" Fental asks.

"It went great. Both Zor and Brickman will be joining us in about an hour." Her sly smile returning to her face.

The next hour passes by routinely as Atany and her crew patiently wait for their new arrivals.

"Captain," Roeton says, "I'm receiving a message from the station. Professors Zor and Brickman are ready to beam over."

"Great. Contact the transporter room and let me know when they are aboard." Less than a minute passes.

"Transporter room reports both are aboard." Roeton reports.

"Very good." Atany replies. "Is there any way you can override the internal communications array so I can broadcast a message on all channels and show this ship on all their monitors?"

"No problem, captain. It'll take about two minutes." Roeton tells her.

"Do it." She orders.

"Channel open, captain." Roeton says. "If it has a speaker, your voice will be heard and every monitor will display this ship."

Atany stands and takes a few steps away from the command chair. She turns to face the main viewscreen.

"This is Captain Dinema Atany of the starship Tartarus. We are currently recruiting crewmen for our ship and our mission. Our mission is that of galactic peace through superior firepower. Anyone wishing to join our cause please contact this ship in the next ten minutes. Thank you." She motions to Roeton to close communications.

● ● ●

Ten minutes pass with fourteen people wishing to join the Tartarus crew. The ten minute countdown hits zero and Atany turns to Roeton.

"Have all the people from the station beamed over?"

"Transporter room reports the last of them are beaming over now."

"Tactical, lock all weapons on that station." Everyone on the bridge pause what they are doing.

"Weapons locked." Lieutenant Commander Sacar says with hesitation in his voice. Atany turns and faces Sacar after hearing the oddness in his voice.

"Don't think about the people on station as innocent." She tells him. "They are enemies. They know our secret and must not be allowed to tell anyone before we inform the quadrant. Got it? Can you handle it?"

"Yes, ma'am, I believe I can." He replies.

"Good answer." She says with a smile. "Now… Fire!" Her tone cold and unfeeling.

Sacar hits the button and eight energy bolts launch from the front of the two weapons nacelles. It takes several seconds for the bolts to reach their targets.

The first two bolts hit the deuterium hull, exploding through to the outermost labs. The second two impact just to the right of the first two, creating an even bigger hull breach. The entire station rocks violently as internal explosions start randomly from ruptured power conduits.

The third two bolts hit deeper inside the station, causing power outages throughout. The fourth set of bolts blast the interior of the station at a point where the research section connects to the support services section, which contains sleeping quarters, administrative offices and food and energy production. The station breaks apart, each section studded with brilliant explosions. In a matter of seconds the research station is obliterated, leaving nothing but rubble and corpses. The death toll is at approximately seven hundred and fifty beings.

"Levi, set a course for Brantax Three. Warp six." Atany says.

"Course laid in. E.T.A. nineteen hours." Levi answers. The image on the screen suddenly becomes streaks of light.

"Captain's log, stardate 30322.32. We are approaching the Brantax star system. Our intent: locate Hawking's associates at the dig site where we started this adventure. Zor and Brickman are hard at work. They're acting like kids in a toy store, which is very good. They are making strides in figuring out the new systems. The other crewmembers are filling in the ranks and relieving a lot of burden."

"Levi, put us in a geosynchronous orbit above the Maroonna dig site and maintain orbit at two hundred kilometers." Atany orders.

"Aye, captain." He replies as he complies. It only takes a few minutes to get there.

"We are now two hundred kilometers above the Maroonna dig site."

"Very good." Atany says softly, calmly. "Roeton, get me the transporter room." She continues.

"Go ahead, captain." Roeton answers.

"Set the transporter to beam a landing party to the coordinates that Hawking, Fental and I beamed up from on our last visit here."

"It'll take a few minutes to recall the data but I'll be ready." Comes from the intercom.

The door to the transporter room opens and Atany, Fental, Hawking and Daniel enter and proceed directly to the platform.

"Energize." The captain orders and in seconds the four find themselves several rooms away from the chamber where Atany and Fental first met Hawking.

"Shawn!" Hawking shouts. His voice echoes several times throughout the mammoth structure. Half a minute passes with no reply.

"Shawn!" He screams even louder. The echoes last a bit longer.

"Ari?" A distant-sounding voice answers in the dimly lit chambers.

"Is that you?" The voice seems closer. "Stand by." It takes nearly two minutes for the shadows of the research team to come into view in the chamber opening adjacent to the one they are in.

"Where the hell are they?" Atany asks after nearly another minute.

"These chambers are very tricky with sound. They'll be here momentarily." Hawking tells her. A few seconds pass and Shawn comes around the corner along with two other people that had not been present during the last visit.

"Shawn!" Hawking shouts with a smile, taking his hand and shaking it vigorously.

"How did the mission go? And what's with the uniform?" Shawn asks with a smile of his own. Hawking looks at the other two with him. He catches on.

"Oh, Ari, let me introduce Doctor Rola Tora." Shawn says, pointing to the man to right. "He is a cryptolinguist, and Doctor Kayla Bourne, our newest Forzak scholar." Pointing to the unattractive woman to his left. "She has some rather unique theories so I figured I'd give her a shot to try and prove or disprove them." Doctor Bourne is from Mylar. The physical attributes of Mylarians are not at all attractive. Hawking looks at Atany, who slowly nods her head in approval.

"That's why we're here, Shawn." Hawking tells him, the excitement bursting through his words. "We found it, Shawn. We really found it."

"You found?" Shawn looks hopeful as he asks.

"The Forzak homeworld, Shawn. We were there." A slight laugh slips through his lips. Tora and Bourne stand silently wide-eyed.

"Are you absolutely sure? You're not just fucking with me?"

"Come with us. See for yourself." He says to his friend. Atany sees the look of longing in the eyes of the other two.

"You two can come along as long as you can contribute to the cause." Atany tells them. Without thinking, both agree.

"Atany to Tartarus, seven to beam up." She says into her communicator. The seven sparkle away.

The transporter cycle completes and the seven are standing on the platform. Atany leads the way out of the transporter room and the six others follow.

"Tell me about what you've found." Shawn asks Hawking as they walk down the hall. "I've imagined the possibilities. You've been there. Tell me, Ari." The excitement in his voice bursting through.

"I'll tell you all about it once we're on the bridge." He tells Shawn.

The group approaches the turbolift and the door opens. In a matter of seconds the door opens again and the group steps onto the bridge. Atany and Fental take their seats in the center of the room. Daniel goes to his science station while Hawking goes to the station he usually works at, followed by his friend and two new associates.

Shawn, Rola and Kayla stand silently, looking around the bridge in awe. Several long seconds pass as the three take in their new surroundings. Shawn shakes his head briskly several times. He sits in the chair by his friend.

"So, Ari," Shawn starts, "What did you find on the Forzak homeworld?"

"I'll answer all your questions in just a second." He answers without lifting his eyes from the screen he's been working on since they've been back. He finishes his work and looks at Shawn, motioning for him to look at the screen.

"Look at this, Shawn." Hawking motions for his friend to look at the screen. The image is the Tartarus. A three view schematic of the ship showing front view, side view and top view along with its statistics.

"What am I looking at?" Shawn asks.

"It's the specs for this ship." He answers.

"Why are you showing me this?"

"We didn't stay on the Forzak homeworld very long." Hawking explains. "We collected a lot of data but our ship was damaged beyond repair and we were looking for a way home."

"This isn't the ship you went there with?" Curiosity fills his face.

"No." He answers with wide eyes and a large grin.

"Then this is?" Shawn's mind is running a mile a minute.

"Yes." He answers almost giddy.

"This ship is Forzak?" Enlightenment shinning on his face.

"Yes." He answers again.

"This is Forzak?" Doctor Tora repeats unbelieving.

"That would make this ship over a thousand years old." Doctor Bourne says with astonishment. "How is it still operational?"

"We have people working on that now, as well as trying to figure out what things on this ship do."

"I think we can help with that part." Tora says.

"What do you mean?" Hawking asks. Atany and Fental turn and look at the four after hearing Tora's remark, their curiosity peaked.

"I'm a cryptolinguist, I study dead languages. Bourne here, knows as much about the Forzak as anyone outside of the two of you." He gestures to Hawking and Shawn.

"I think they would be useful in engineering working with Zor and Brickman." Atany interrupts when Tora finishes.

"How can they help there?" Fental asks.

"Well, Zor and Brickman know the science. These three know the language and the culture. They can translate the glyphs and help decipher anything else that Zor and Brickman can't figure out."

"I'll bring them down to engineering, captain." Hawking volunteers.

"Do it." Atany orders. The four leave the bridge.

"Levi," Atany says after the turbolift door closes, "set a course for Spaceport 3. Warp seven."

"Course plotted and laid in, Captain. ETA eight point three hours."

"Go," she orders. The screen turns to streaking stars once again.

Hawking enters the drive section with the three newest crew-members in tow. They head straight to Benjamin, who is trying to translate glyphs that are currently on the monitor on the main inter-face computer located in the isle at the far end of the engines.

"Lieutenant Commander Benjamin," Hawking shouts as they approach him from behind, "This is Professor Shawn Rytell." He motions to his friend and continues to the other two.

"This is Doctor Rola Tora and Doctor Kayla Bourne. They are here to assist in translating and deciphering the Forzak glyphs."

"Welcome aboard." Benjamin says as he shakes both of their hands.

"I can use all the help you can offer."

"Just let us know what you need." Bourne says.

"I must return to the bridge." Hawking tells the four. "Hook them up with Zor and Brickman. They should be able to help speed up the translations you need down here." Hawking leaves the four and heads back to the bridge.

• • •

The turbolift door opens and Hawking steps onto the bridge, taking his seat. All is quiet. He starts going over the specs on the vortex device.

An hour passes with nothing of interest occurring. The blare of the yellow alert klaxon breaks the normal humming and beeping from the various consoles.

"Report," Atany orders calmly.

"Scanning," Daniel replies. After several seconds he continues, "It's an Orancaran resort ship. Distance one point five light years."

"Full of people enjoying a vacation?" She says somewhat resentful.

"Affirmative. Scans show one thousand, seventy-five people on board."

"What are you thinking, Captain?" Fental asks with concern.

"Supplies, Dutona, that's what I'm thinking." Atany answers with the matter-of-fact tone that bothers Fental. "They have enough food and booze and medical supplies, as well as other provisions that we will be running out of soon, for all those people, for how long, what, three or four weeks? How long will that last us? It's all there for the taking."

"What, exactly, are you saying, Captain?"

"A boarding party," she answers. "Anyone got a problem with that?"

Everyone replies, though some hesitantly, in the negative.

"I didn't think so," she says, looking around the large room.

"Helm," she continues, "set an intercept course. Bring us one hundred kilometers dead in front of them. Lieutenant Jullian, activate the Horatha invisibility shield."

"Aye, Captain." He says with concern, though not as evident as Fental.

"ETA two point two minutes."

● ● ●

The battle cruiser sweeps in a large arc and comes head to head with the Orancaran resort ship, parking one hundred kilometers in front of her. Once in place, the Tartarus matches course and speed, maintaining the one hundred kilometer buffer ordered by the captain.

Atany sits in her chair staring at the ship on the screen, knowing none of the one thousand, seventy-five souls on board her have any idea what is directly in their path. She sits silent for several more seconds.

"Jullian," she says somewhat softly, "deactivate the invisibility shield."

The captain and his bridge crew are maintaining normal speed and course. All systems show everything is normal, everything is quiet.

"Holy fuck!" the helmsman screams in panic as he puts all thrusters on full to stop his ship.

"What is it?" the captain says as he turns and sees his helmsman's eyes bulging from his head. He follows the terrified helmsman's glare and looks out of the huge window in the front of the bridge.

The captain, along with the rest of the bridge crew, sees, within a distortion field, the semi-solid image of the Forzak battle cruiser. It takes only a few seconds for the Tartarus to become fully visible.

"All stop!" The captain of the resort ship screams.

"All stop! The helmsman screams back as he adjusts the controls. Before the Orancaran ship can completely stop, Daniel and Voltarus materialize on the bridge, phaser rifles in hand.

Phaser beams take out the helmsman, the navigator and the other two men on the bridge. Before the captain can react, Daniel is standing two inches in front of him. The captain knows his crew is no match for the strangers who just took his bridge. Daniel takes out his communicator.

"Nire, report," Daniel says.

"Nire, here. Engineering is secure." The disembodied voice of the female archangel medic sounds on the bridge.

"Now, Captain," Daniel says calmly yet sternly. "Here is what's going to happen. I have four people in engineering. Right now two of them are heading to the galley. We are requisitioning your food stores, all of them."

"L.C.," Voltarus interrupts, "passenger and crew lists and cargo manifest on screens."

"Great." Daniel replies. He turns his attention back to the captain and continues, "Now that my associate has gotten the computer info, you and he are going to the ship's vault. You will follow his instructions to the letter or he will kill you." He smiles politely as he finishes.

Voltarus nudges the captain with the muzzle of his assault rifle. The captain turns to Voltarus with defiance in his motions. Voltarus' cold eyes pierce back at him emotionless. The captain submits and the two walk toward the door at the back of the bridge as Daniel walks over and studies the data on the two screens.

About fifteen minute pass when Daniel's communicator beeps.

"Daniel here," He says into the box.

"Fental, here," the first officer's voice sounds. "We'll be done with the food stores in minutes. What do you want us to take next?"

"Focus on the two aft cargo bays on the port side. By the time you're done that, Voltarus should be done in the vault so contact him next. I'll be in touch as soon as I verify something."

"Will do," Fental tells him. "Remember, Daniel, watch the clock."

"Affirmative," he tells her. He puts his communicator away and leaves the bridge.

* * *

Daniel stands in front of the double doors leading into the main casino. He walks into the room and looks around. Not seeing what he is looking for, he heads to the ship's theater.

Daniel sees his target in the third row on the right side. He walks to the isle behind the last row of seats unnoticed. He takes a deep breath and raises his rifle slowly. He aims and fires a rapid volley.

Three of the five actors on the stage are systematically thrown back as they are hit by the rounds fired by Daniel. They are dead before they hit the ground.

In a panic, people start to stand, trying to run. Daniel fires a volley of shots into the ceiling. Everyone freezes in place, seeing that Daniel has the only access point blocked.

"Everyone shut up!" Daniel screams. It takes a few seconds for the room to go silent. He waits until he has everyone's attention.

"Would Sandy Holt please step forward," He says loudly but politely. No one answers. Daniel waits for a full minute. There is still no reply.

He raises the assault rifle and fires several rounds from the hip. One of the energy bolt hits the middle-aged man in the tuxedo standing two meters in front of him square in the chest. The other two hit the woman standing beside him, one in the chest and one in the face. They fly backward forcefully, sending people behind them to the ground. Those who witnessed the murders start screaming. Daniel fires three more shots into the ceiling again, and, again, the room goes quiet.

"Please, Ambassador Holt," Daniel says with his smile back on his face. "Let's avoid any more loss of life. Please come forward." In just under a minute the crowd in front of him separates and, from between them steps a beautiful red-haired woman, flanked by two large men in plain black suits. Daniel smiles as he takes her hand, kissing it.

"Hello, Ambassador Holt. My name is Lieutenant Commander Daniel of the starship Tartarus. Please excuse my methods but your presence aboard our ship is hereby requested."

"If you would have followed proper protocols, my staff would have considered an appointment, but after this display you can go fuck yourself." She answers with surprising composure.

"With all due respect, madam Ambassador, but I must insist." The smile on his face widens as he lifts the barrel of his rifle, aiming it at her face. He sees the panic spread across her face.

"Please, Ambassador, I said you are needed on the ship." He tells her as he moves his weapon slightly to her left and right, firing two shots. The smile on his face never leaves as the two rounds hit the men that came forward with the ambassador, killing both of them instantly.

Using his rifle, he motions her into the hall. He follows her as he points his rifle at the crowd. He takes out his communicator.

"Two to beam up." He says and the two dematerialize.

Daniel steps out of the turbolift and stands by Atany.

"Are we done with this ship?" She says to Daniel.

"Yes," he answers. "I brought a guest back with me. Ambassador Sandy Holt."

"Of Holt Defensive Arms?" She asks.

"The same," he answers.

"Where is she?"

"Lieutenant Commander Nire is giving her the once over."

"I hope she enjoys it." The captain says of the ambassador.

"Nire loves this part."

"Levi, back us away from that ship. Best possible speed." Atany says, "Sacar, when we're at a safe distance, get rid of her."

The Tartarus starts to back away from the resort ship. It takes about a minute and a half for the ship to reach a safe distance. When Sacar reads the appropriate numbers he presses a control on his console. The ship is vaporized in an instant, taking with it one thousand, seventy-four people.

"Captain!" Fental shouts in disbelief. Atany turns her head, still smiling, as the rest of the bridge crew turn their heads at the raised voice. Fental notices and immediately regains her composure.

"Captain," her tone much softer now, "can we speak in private?"

"Sure," The captain answers. "Let's go." The two get up and leave the bridge. They enter the conference room.

"What's on your mind, Fental?" Atany asks.

"With all due respect, captain," Fental starts, "but what the fuck are you thinking?" Her voice escalading.

"You know my plan, Fental."

"That's not what I'm talking about and you know it," anger thick in the first officer's voice. "I'm talking about over a thousand civilians on that ship, not to mention the innocent lives on the research station."

"They were all potential enemies," Atany explains.

"No, captain, not a chance," Fental continues. "Ninety-nine percent of those people would have preferred captivity over death."

"To bad we'll never know," The captain says in her matter-of-fact tone. "But, you know," She continues. "You've given me something to think about."

"What's that?"

"In due time, Fental, in due time," Atany replies as she heads toward the door. "But I need to know," She turns her head to face Fental. "Are you still with me?"

"As long as you have a conscience," She answers.

"No promises," She replies as she exits into the corridor.

Chapter 6

"Captain's log, stardate 30326.83. Our raid on the Orancaran resort ship has yielded enough food for about a year at present compliment, as well as medical supplies. The vault yielded a decent assortment of jewels and gold that we can trade for fuel. Our next stop is Spaceport 3. ETA six point three hours."

The crew rotation finishes and all the night-duty personnel have signed in. Atany remains at her station, as does Daniel.

"ETA six point one hours," Lieutenant Commander Merah reports.

"Excellent," Atany replies. "Maintain course and speed." She says as she signs off on the daily reports. Returning the padds to the yeoman of the watch, she slumps back in her seat.

Fental lays on her bed, unable to fall asleep, the day's events running through her mind. She cannot, in her own conscience, condone or justify the killing of all those innocent people.

• • •

Two decks below and two sections over, Professor Hawking is doing the same. His conscience is keeping him awake, the faces of the dead filling his mind.

Two hours pass and Fental still cannot sleep. She gets up and puts her clothes on. She sluggishly makes her way to the mess hall. Getting a cup of strong coffee, Dutona sits at the table in the corner furthest from the door. She takes a slow, long sip, still lost in thought. A shadow sweeps across her, blocking the light from the room. She looks up.

"Mind if I join you?" Hawking asks.

"Wow," she replies. "You look like I feel."

"Yeah, same to you." He tells her as he sits.

"Thanks." She says. "Why do you feel like I look?"

"Dinema's actions with the resort ship," He confesses.

"Me too," she sips her coffee.

"Can I ask you something personal?" Hawking asks shyly.

"You can ask me anything you want, Professor... I mean Commander."

"Do you think Atany was justified in destroying the Orancaran ship?"

"No, not at all," she answers in a near whisper.

"Neither do I, but I don't know what to do, who to see."

"There's nothing we can do." Fental starts. "On our way to Research Station Alpha Atany told me she intends to gain nothing less than total domination of the quadrant using this ship." Concern weighing heavily on her face.

"I'll tell you what," he begins, speaking as softly as Fental. "We need to keep an eye on her. I know she's already pushing it with some of the crew. Let's see what happens when we get to Spaceport 3."

"What do you intend to do?" She asks cautiously.

"I don't know yet. We have about three and a half hours until we get there. I'll figure something." He tells her.

* * *

"You have to figure something out." She says as she takes his hand, her eyes burning into his.

"I'll figure it out." He tells her, trying to ease her fear and concern. He covers the hand that is on his, with his other, squeezing her hand in a show of comfort. She smiles back brightly at his gesture with genuine appreciation. They stay affixed for several minutes.

"I've got to get some rest," Hawking tells her when he forcibly shakes away the mesmerizing effect of her eyes. "Can I see you later?"

"Of course," she replies as she stands with him. They leave the mess hall, heading toward their individual quarters.

Three hours later finds Fental stepping onto the bridge to find everyone, including Hawking, at their stations. She sits in her seat beside Atany, smiling slightly at the captain.

"Feel better?" Atany asks with a smile.

"Yeah, actually," she answers. "Had a hard time at first but finally feel asleep. I feel really good now. Power naps are the best." She sits back with a continued smile.

"ETA five minutes," Levi volunteers before the captain asks.

"Sacar, are there any other ships in weapons range?" Atany asks.

"There are seven, captain," he reports. "Five cargo transports and two science ships. None are between us and the spaceport."

"I'm not taking any chances." Atany says, showing concern of her own. "Lock weapons on all the ships, just in case." She orders. "Bring us out of warp, Levi."

"Captain, I recommend you put the invisibility shield up now!" Lieutenant Commander Roeton, at the communications console, says with a sense of urgency.

"Explain." Atany asks.

"Engage the shield." Roeton repeats.

"Engage the shield." Atany commands.

* * *

"Invisibility shield activated." Lieutenant Jullian confirms.

"Now, explain." Dinema demands.

"I'm picking up an alpha one priority message from Alliance Command to all Alliance ships."

"About what?" She asks.

"Us," He answers. An eerie silence descends over the bridge. Several minutes pass as everyone overcomes the numbing shock.

"What about us?" She asks with little concern.

"Alliance Command is issuing a warning about an unknown ship. It is of immense size and destructive capabilities. Definitely hostile but of unknown intent. It is a report position alert including a do not approach recommendation." He reports.

"The Alliance was going to find out sooner or later." Fental says.

"Ah, hell, Fental," Atany says after several long seconds of silence. "You're right, of course. What the hell can they do to us?" Fental looks past the captain and focuses on Hawking. He sees the concern in her eyes.

"Keep us here for the time being, Levi." The captain orders.

"All stop." Levi says as he manipulates the controls. Atany sits quietly in her seat contemplating her next move. It takes quite a while.

"Helm, bring us a thousand meters away from the station at one half impulse." She orders calmly. "Open hailing frequencies, like at the research station, every channel on every devise and every monitor showing this ship."

"On it, Captain," Roeton answers. It takes nearly a minute before he answers, "All set, Captain."

"This is Captain Dinema Atany of the starship Tartarus. My ship is in need of some somewhat *exotic* computer components and several engineering technicians to assist in repairs. Compensation will be generous. All interested parties can reach me on frequency…, well, actually, any frequency."

It takes a few minutes before the first call comes in. It is an engineer in need of a better career. The next two calls are also engineers. They are transported to the drive section, and Commander Benjamin.

The next three calls are computer dealers who have a talent for obtaining unique computers, both hardware and software. They are transported to the conference room. Atany stands stiffly.

"Open hailing frequencies again."

"Channel open, Captain."

"Attention Spaceport Three, this is Captain Atany once again. We are also in need of some crewmembers to handle support jobs and we are currently screening potential candidates for such positions. Anyone interested contact my ship. Thanks again." She signals to close channels.

"Channels closed." Roeton reports.

"I'm going to meet with the computer dealers. Do not disturb us. Daniel, Fental, you're with me." Atany says as she walks toward the aft doorway, followed by Daniel and Fental.

"Captain," Roeton says quickly. "Before you go, what about Ambassador Holt?"

"Leave her where she is for now." Atany answers as the three leave the bridge.

The captain and her husband, along with her first officer, enter the conference room to find the three men sitting at the table patiently.

"Hello, gentlemen," Atany says. "I'm sorry it took so long. We were unavoidably delayed." She hands each of them a padd. "This is a list of the specs for the components we need. If you have, or can fabricate, components that match these specs we can do business."

The three men spend several quiet minutes looking over the specs on the padds. Rocca Balathar, the merchant representing the Qualor Group is the first to speak.

"I think I can have some of what you are asking for but it will take about an hour." He tells Atany.

"Very good," she replies with delight.

"Unfortunately, I can't even come close to what you require, Captain." Kalon Decour, from Ultra Corporation, informs the captain.

"I can supply some of your needs as well." Micca Reuben, from System Cybernetics, says last.

"Okay, then, gentlemen." Atany starts with a smile. "Mister Decour, my first officer will escort you to the transporter room. Daniel will stay with you two and coordinate the deal. I must return to my duties." She leaves the room as Daniel sits and Fental escorts Decour.

Atany steps back onto the bridge and takes her seat. She stares at the viewscreen, quietly contemplating her next move. An hour passes and there is no reply from Daniel. She waits patiently. Thirty more minutes pass before Daniel enters the bridge.

"Are we set?" She asks.

"Yeah, we managed to get comparable components for everything on the list."

"That's good news. While you were doing that we brought four new crewmen aboard for support work and three more engineers." She adds.

"Then everything we needed to do here has been accomplished."

"We can leave whenever you're ready, Captain." Fental says.

Atany turns to Sacar, who is focused on her. She nods to him and he presses a button on his panel. In the blink of an eye Research Station 3 goes from matter to elemental, exploding in a brilliant flash of light. The ship rocks slightly.

The explosion takes out two of the transports at the station. The other five ships go to warp before the shockwave hits them. All that's left is a debris field where the station used to be.

● ● ●

"What the fuck did you do that for?!" Fental screams as she stands. "Are you insane?!"

"Just a little, I guess." Atany answers with a giggle. "I'm looking at the bigger picture."

"What could be bigger than the thousands of lives you've taken since we found this ship?"

"How about the sixty-three worlds in our quadrant?" Atany answers with her own question. "That totals about what, forty trillion people? Bringing a peaceful coexistence to all that is the bigger picture."

"Your bigger picture still doesn't justify the lives you've taken." Fental continues. "There was no reason to destroy the research station or the spaceport or the Orancaran resort ship! You've gone off the deep end."

"Fental," Atany says calmly, "sit down and calm down. You need to get a grip."

"I need to get a grip?" Fental says slightly more calm. "I didn't order the execution of all those people."

"You need to understand, given time, these people would have to fight against us. I just took a proactive stance."

"Relax, Fental." Sacar shouts from his station.

"It's all part of the job." Daniel adds.

Fental's head starts to spin. *Can I be the only one who thinks this is wrong?* She thinks to herself as she looks over at Hawking. He nods his head slightly left to right, hoping she can see the meaning on his face.

Dutona notices his gesture and expression. She forces herself to calm down and sit. She takes a deep breath and lets it out slowly.

"I'm sorry, Captain." She says apologetically. "I wasn't expecting that."

"No worries, Fental. I knew you'd come around quickly." Atany replies. "With the quadrant under my rule, the lives we save from preventing future wars will far exceed the loss of life thus far."

"I see your perspective." Fental says, saving herself.

• • •

"I knew you would." Atany tells her as she takes her first officer's hand.

Hawking sits back with a sigh of relief.

"Helm, lay in a course for Horath, warp one." Atany orders.

"Course and speed plotted and laid in." Levi responds. "ETA twenty-two hours. Engaging." The stars start streaking by.

"Why are we going to Horath?" Fental asks

"The Horatha are our greatest risk." Atany answers. "We are going to neutralize that risk."

The rest of the duty shift goes by uneventful. Fental steps off of the turbolift down the hall from her quarters. She gets half way down the hall when she hears the turbolift door open again. She turns.

"Fental, got a minute?" Commander Hawking asks as he jogs toward her. "We need to discuss what happened."

"I've got twelve hours." She answers with a huge gorgeous smile. "Let's go in my quarters." She suggests.

"They continue down the hall several dozen meters until a door on the right slides open. The two enter.

"Would you like a drink?" She asks Hawking as she walks to the rectangular computer console on a small table against the wall.

"Sure," he says as he sits on the sofa in the middle of the room. "Whatever you're having is fine."

"Two cylerium nyborgs, twenty ounce, thirty-six degrees," She says to the alien machine. The top of the rectangle starts to glow as two cylinders begin to appear from spiraling sparkles of light.

"It took a little while but I found the replicator. I programmed it with a few of my favorites. I think you'll like this one." She tells him as she walks to the sofa. She hands him the glass as she sits beside him.

"You need to know that I said nothing on the bridge because of the number of supporters Atany has up there." Hawking confesses.

"That's what I figured." She also confesses. "That's why I played along, though it was hard."

"We'll figure out what to do about her but we've got to be very careful. Personally, I don't want to see the outer door of an airlock, if you know what I mean." Hawking says and sips his drink.

"We've still got a while," Fental says, "most important right now is relaxing. Something will come to us." She slides closer to her guest. "I don't know about you, but I need some serious relaxation." There's a noticeable quiver in her voice.

"I know exactly what you mean." Hawking replies with the same quiver in his voice. He leans in close, putting his hand on the nape of her neck. He pulls her in, locking his lips to hers. She puts up no resistance as she thrusts her tongue around his. Their kiss lasts a long time as they press their bodies tighter together.

"Wow!" Hawking whispers as their lips part, both trying to get their breaths back.

"Yep." Fental agrees several breaths later. She pulls him in for another kiss. She starts to moan as he takes control and caresses her breasts with a firm yet gentle grip. It takes only a few seconds before Hawking lifts her uniform tunic over her head.

Their kiss continues strongly as Hawking tries to unhook Fental's bra. Several seconds pass.

"Can you unlock this, please?" Hawking asks with a smile.

"Having problems, Professor?" She says after she laughs, all along unhooking the clips on her bra.

He pulls her in for another kiss as his hand slides gently under her. His hand caresses her breasts firmly. His fingers find her nipple and he pinches it until she moans deeply under his control.

Fental's hand slides down Hawking's arm and drops to his thigh. As he continues to caress her breast, Fental moves her hand up his thigh until she finds his now erect cock. She grips it as best she can through his trousers and starts to slide her hand up and down along the length of his shaft.

A dozen of Fental's strokes has Hawking turning his body, causing Fental to lose her grip. He breaks their kiss with a smile.

"I'm sorry but I really want to fuck you and if you keep doing that I'm going to get off way to soon." He says as he starts to slide her slacks off. She smiles back at him as he slides her panties off and throws them off to the side.

Hawking kneels in front of Dutona, her legs spread out before him. He lifts her left leg up from her ankle and raises it until it reaches his lips. Ari's lips caress Fental's calf and gently, slowly work toward her knee.

He rests her leg on his shoulder and, as he continues to run his tongue along her skin he caresses her thigh, using both hands to sensually massage both the inside and outside of her thigh. She moans deeply as his hand nears her now wet pussy.

While his tongue darts around the back of her knee, he starts rubbing her right thigh with his left hands as the right hand caresses the upper left thigh, wrapping his hand around the muscle, his fingers brushing her pussy lips. He hears her moans deepen and keeps his right fingers inches away from her pink, hairless slit.

Hawking slides onto his stomach as he continues to message her thigh with his tongue. He squeezes her thighs lightly as he lightly rubs the outer edges of her wet pussy flesh with his thumbs. His tongue approaches Fental's love tunnel and her moans grow louder. Her legs start to move uncontrollably as the fire inside her burns out of control.

When his tongue reaches her pussy he gently parts her lips with his fingers as he runs his tongue along the edge of her clit. Her thighs tighten around his head as her body convulses into orgasmic spasms. He darts his tongue around her clit as he slips a thumb inside of her.

After several thrusts with his thumb, Fental grabs Hawking by the hair and pulls him up. She stares him dead in the eye.

"I want you inside me." She says with mock seriousness.

• • •

"Soon," He says and puts his face back down between her legs. He takes her clit between his lips and slides it in his mouth. He continues to slide her clit in and out for several more seconds before she grabs at his hair again.

He releases her clit and kisses up to her navel. He darts his tongue around her navel as his fingers slide in and out of her. She moans more loudly as she grinds her hips around his thrusting fingers.

As Hawking continues to thrust two fingers deep inside of Dutona, he kisses his way to the nipple of her right breast, flicking it with his tongue over and over again. Fental twists her body as a message to Hawking. He acknowledges.

Hawking rolls on top of Dutona. He looks her dead in the eyes, with a gentle smile. She grabs his rock hard shaft and guides it to the entrance of her burning hot pussy. He slowly inserts his cock the full length, Fental's eyes growing bigger with each inch that enters her.

He locks his lips to Fental's, forcing his tongue into her mouth. She takes it in willingly, enjoying every second. As their tongues dance together, Hawking slides his cock out to the tip. He playfully thrusts his cock in two inches then withdraws. He does this several times in quick repetition. He pauses for half a second then

Hawking reaches up with his right hand and, from behind her left shoulder, grabs a handful of hair, pulling it hard. Her head cocks back as he breaks their kiss and starts running his tongue along her neck.

While thrusting his cock hard into her pussy, his tongue reaches her earlobe, sucking on it and his left hand finds her nipple. He pinches it firmly, twisting it lightly, back and forth, with his fingers. This combination of stimulations causes Fental's body to explode in orgasmic ecstasy.

Hawking continues to thrust his cock in and out with rhythmic fury, bringing Dutona to orgasm again in minutes. Several

● ● ●

minutes after that he feels her body building up for yet another orgasm. As her next orgasm builds, Hawking feels his starting to build. Her body starts to tighten up, preparing to explode. Hawking starts to thrust faster as he begins to orgasm. Suddenly Dutona explodes along with Hawking. Their final, simultaneous orgasms lasts what seems like forever. He rolls off and scoops her in his arms and without a word both drift off to sleep.

Nine hours later finds our two lovers waking up together, both grinning from ear to ear. Hawking give Fental a long, passionate kiss.

"Wonderful stuff, that cylerium nyborg," He says with a smile.

"Sure is," She smile back and returns his kiss.

"We've got to get ready and get to the bridge." She says.

"I know." He replies. "I'm going to take a shower." He gets out of bed and heads toward the bathroom.

While Hawking is washing his face he feels hands, from behind, gently messaging his cock. He feels his erection rise quickly. He rinses the soap from his eyes in time to see Fental come around to his front.

He spins her around and bends her over at the waist. As the shower rains down on Fental's head, Hawking enters her from behind. Fental orgasms after ten minutes. Another five minutes brings her second. With her second, Hawking cums with her.

"Now that's the way to start the day." She says while she washes his back.

"Absolutely right," He agrees. They finish washing and drying each other.

"How about lunch?" Hawking asks while they get dressed.

"Sounds good," Fental answers.

They finish dressing and head out into the hall. They take the turbolift to the bridge to find Merah, Richards and Borkin at the helm stations. The rest of the night duty rotation are at their stations.

How long until we reach Horath?" She asks as she takes her seat. Hawking heads quietly to the science station he's been calling home.

"One point eight hours." Merah answers.

"Thank you." She replies. She looks over to Hawking, who smiles when their eyes make contact. She returns his smile with one of her own.

Twenty minutes pass when the turbolift door opens. Atany and Daniel come onto the bridge and take their seats quickly and quietly.

"One point five hours to Horath." Merah offers the captain.

"Very good," Atany answers then looks at Fental. "Good morning, Dutona." She adds.

"Good morning, Dinema." Fental says with a smile.

"How are you this morning?" Atany asks.

"Excellent." Fental answers.

"Glad to hear it." Atany replies as she turns and faces the main viewscreen, the smile melting off of her face.

"Captain, we are being hailed on Alliance frequency Alpha." Lieutenant Commander Reuben says in an odd tone. "It's Procouncil Jacorrian."

"On screen," The captain orders and the fat sisarcian is now on the main viewer. He looks very angry.

"What the fuck do you think you're doing!?" Jacorrian screams uncontrollably, the veins in his neck and forehead pulsing with every syllable.

"Good day to you, AtTionne." Atany answers with a smile, oblivious to his anger. "What are you referring to?"

"Are you insane!?" He continues screaming.

"You need to be precise." She says calmly, happily.

"Putting the Alliance at war with the Rillians, the Horatha and the Orancarans! The destruction of the research station and the spaceport! So I'll ask you again, are you fucking insane!?" Still screaming.

"It's all self-defense and self-preservation." She tells him.

"Justify that line of bullshit! Now!" Screaming with a tone of disbelief, disbelief in what she just said.

"Well, first off, we discovered the Forzak homeworld. When we returned through the vortex, the Rillians were waiting for us. The Rillian ambassador hired saboteurs, by the way." She says matter-of-factly and continues, "The Horatha had technology that we needed so we took it. We needed supplies from the two stations so we took what we needed."

"What about the Orancaran ship!? What did you need from them!?" He continues screaming uncontrollably.

"Target practice." She answers with a smile. A look of stunned disbelief spreads across his face while he tries to find his voice. It takes him a few seconds.

"You are fucking nuts!?" He screams back at her.

"No, Procouncil, what I am is the captain of the most powerful battleship in the galaxy and with the quadrant under my control there will be no more wars, no more violence. We will at last be at peace." She retorts.

"We're coming for you, Atany, with all we can muster, we're coming for you!?" He screams with slightly more calmness, slightly more.

"Well, in just over an hour we'll be arriving at Horath. See you there, if you can make it. Good health, AtTionne." She says, still smiling, and signals Reuben to close the channel and he does. The main viewscreen goes back to the streaking stars of warp drive.

Chapter 7

"Captain's log, stardate 30385.09. We are entering the Horatha star system. We don't know what to expect but I'm anticipating an easy victory. We'll find out in a matter of minutes."

"Tactical showing automated defense drones three thousand kilometers ahead. Scanners show seventy-two, evenly spaced out, covering a span of four trillion square kilometers." Lieutenant Commander Sacar says, now that the day shift has come on duty. The night rotation crewmen are still on the bridge at auxiliary stations, curious about what's about to happen.

"Helm, change course to three, five, zero mark zero, one, five. Reduce speed to three quarter impulse." Atany orders.

"Course changed, Captain." Levi says as the stars on the screen change direction.

"Speed to three quarter impulse." Lieutenant Torres informs the captain as the stars suddenly become static.

• • •

"Tactical, lock all weapons on as many of those drones as you can per volley and let loose as they come to bear." She commands.

"Aye, Captain." Comes from both Sacar and Lieutenant Hoon. Three minutes pass, eerily silent.

"Torpedoes away," Sacar says, ending the silence.

"Phasers firing." Hoon follows.

"Sixteen destroyed." Sacar says. "Locking on. Firing. Thirty-two gone." Sacar continues.

"Keep it up." Atany says. Just then the ship shimmies slightly as the main viewscreen blinks."

"What was that?" The captain requests.

"Checking." Daniel says as he spins to face his station. "Eight Horatha warships coming up on our six." He answers.

"Sacar, get rid of those ships." Atany orders. "Hoon, you continue with those drones." The ship shimmies again.

"I can't get a weapon's lock." Sacar tell Atany. "I'll have to fire manually."

"Do your best just get them off our back." She commands.

"You got it, Captain." He answers her. He starts firing torpedoes as the ships outside maneuver around the deadly bolts.

Three of the first eight torpedoes hit the lead Horatha ship, destroying its invisibility shields, plasma venting from its port nacelle. The other seven ships open fire at the massive starship, their entire combined volley hitting the Tartarus on the top of the drive section, at the base of the upper tee shaped structure, weakening the shields enough to cause breaches on several decks.

"Are those bulkheads holding?" Atany asks.

"Internal sensors showing the bulkheads are holding." Hawking, at the auxiliary science station, answers. "But the structural integrity of the entire section has been compromised."

"How are you doing with those drones?" She asks.

"Two more volleys and we can pass through the net safely."

"Stay on it. Helm, set a course through the safe zone, full impulse."

"Course plotted and laid in." Levi says after a few seconds.

"Get this thing moving." Atany says.

"Engines engaged." Torres replies.

The ship turns slightly to the left as the engines kick in. As it moves forward, the Horatha warships fall in behind the alien ship. The Forzak battleship suddenly fires several full volleys behind them and a wall of twenty-four torpedoes and eight phaser beams separate the hunted from the hunters.

Three of the Horatha warships cannot escape the wall of death and are obliterated.

"Bring us to zero, nine, zero mark." Atany says with a bit more confidence. "Reduce speed to half impulse." The ship turns right and slows down, the Horatha following suit.

"We'll be in range of the drones in fifteen seconds." Sacar shouts.

"Maintain course and speed." She replies.

"Ten seconds." Sacar continues. "Five seconds... now in range." Before Sacar finishes his sentence the viewscreen is filled with hundreds of energy bolts blindly seeking their target.

"Increase speed to full impulse now." Atany says sternly. "Fire four volleys aft, on my mark." She continues. "And now, fire!"

"Firing." Sacar and Hoon reply to her order.

"Two ships gone," Daniel says after a few seconds. "The last two ships are disengaging and retreating.

"Good." Atany says. "Hard to port then set a course for Horath."

"Yes, Captain." Levi says and quickly complies. The huge ship turns hard left and, after several seconds, gets out of range of the remaining drones.

"We'll reach Horath in twelve minutes at present speed." Levi informs Atany.

"Very good, maintain." She responds as she looks over at Fental who meets her with a smile.

"Good job, Atany." She says happily. "That was very slick."

"Thanks. I'm glad you're with me." Atany says, smiling back as she focuses her attention to the main viewscreen.

"Nowhere else, Captain." Fental says as the smile leaves her face while her eyes lock with Hawking, who nods with acceptance. She sends him a light smile which he promptly returns.

"We're passing Horath's outer moon." Levi says aloud.

"Tactical, report." The captain orders.

"There is a satellite array around the center moon." Sacar begins. "There are also two bases on the inner moon."

"Levi, get us to the center moon."

"One minute, Captain."

"Sacar, lock on to that satellite array and take it out."

The mammoth vessel approaches the small moon with their stolen invisibility shield at full power. Everything seems normal as the Tartarus closes in. There is no sign that they've been picked up on any scanners.

"Firing phasers." Hoon announces as the energy beams emerge from the sides of the viewscreen, heading toward the moon. A second and a half passes when the bridge crew see eight tiny explosions above the surface of the moon.

A second round of beams emerge from the sides of the viewscreen and in the same second and a half eight more tiny explosions. When the flashes fade the satellite array, responsible for protecting the Horatha homeworld, is nothing but a pile of twisted metal debris.

"Oops," Hoon says sarcastically. "Now they're blind and deaf."

"Okay, then," Atany continues. "Get us to the inner moon."

"ETA five minutes," Levi informs her. The crew sit back and wait. A few minutes pass before the moon comes into view. A few minutes later and the Tartarus is in firing range.

* * *

"Sacar, take out that base." Her words deliberate and cold. With no words said, a round of phaser fire along with eight photon torpedoes appear on the screen.

Just over a second after the eight phaser beams hit their marks, the shields protecting the base glow with the impact of the first two torpedoes. With the third impact, the glow of the shields flickers out as small explosions at various points around the base. The rest of the torpedoes strike the exterior metal walls of the base causing large explosions around the base.

As the bridge crew watches the explosions ripple through the Horatha base, Atany's smile grows wider, brighter, with each new blast.

"All weapons, open fire." Atany says with conviction. The screen fills with eight long beams of phaser fire followed by sixteen torpedoes heading toward the destination.

Suddenly there appears four explosions on the exterior of the base, indicating the destruction of the shield generators was successful. Four more explosions appear on the base, quickly followed by four more. The last four hit quickly after the previous ones, all exploding in different places.

"Readings?" Atany asks as she turns to face Daniel.

"Eighty-five percent of the base is uninhabitable. Life signs are sporadic but do register on sensors.

"Move to the other base." Atany orders.

"We'll be in range in two minutes." Levi says. As the moon slowly rotates on the viewscreen, it takes a minute and a half before the base comes into view on the horizon.

"Fire when we're in range." The captain commands. Seconds later torpedoes and phaser bolts shoot from the ship. The shields flicker.

"Again," She says and this volley knocks out the shield generators and exposes the base.

Without a word another round of death launches from the Forzak battleship. The impacts are over the whole base, causing explosions throughout the complex.

"Sensors show sporadic life signs throughout the base," Daniel reports. "One more round ought to do it." He suggests.

"Fire another volley." Atany says with some annoyance in her voice. The weapons of destruction hurl toward the remnants of the base. After three seconds they make impact and explosions riddle the remains.

"That does it." Daniel informs the captain. "No life signs, no power emissions, nothing."

"Levi, set a course for Horath." Atany orders. "Full impulse."

"ETA three point two minutes." Lieutenant Torres tells her.

"Tactical, I want phasers to concentrate on military centers. I want photons to lock on industrial targets." Atany continues. "Leave civilian population centers alone. Is that okay with you, Fental?" Dutona nods in agreement.

The ship enters orbit undetected. It makes two complete orbits, scanning the surface of a world no one on the ship has ever seen.

"Targeting scanners have detected all the complexes you specified," Sacar tells Atany. "Ready on your command."

"Fire at will," Atany says. Volley after volley of weapon's fire rains down on the unsuspecting planet below. Six volleys leave the ship before the first one hits the ground. Little round fireballs appear on the surface in sporadic locations, quickly spreading across the visible land masses.

The ship orbits the planet four times without letting up on their assault. The surface is pitted with black blotches that used to be various structures, now burned out, smoldering skeletons.

"I'm picking up three ships, on an intercept course, coming in from the planet." Sacar tell the captain.

"They must have their invisibility shields on." Atany says as there is nothing showing on the screen. "We can play that game too. Engage the Horatha invisibility shields."

"Shields engaged." Lieutenant Jullian replies.

"Enemy ships slowed down." Daniel says. "They may not be able to read us."

"That's good… if it's correct." Atany says. "Lock on those ships and blast them to hell."

The weapons appear on the screen, heading in different directions. The weapons fade off ahead of the ship, leaving just the tan and brown orb called Horath floating in the vastness of space.

Three flashes appear on the screen, followed by the dim glows of the weapons impacting on the shields of the cloaked warships. Three more flashes reveal the hidden warships as their shield generators fail.

"Fire!" Atany says with excitement. The weapons make impact on the ships and they are instantaneously vaporized. The huge battleship continues along its path toward the Horatha homeworld.

"Is there anything else on tactical?" Atany asks calmly.

"All clear, Captain," Sacar says. Several seconds pass. "Correction, two more warships coming into range from behind the planet."

"Fire at will," Atany commands. "As they come to bear." The same scenario plays out as before. As the final volley heads toward the Horatha warships the unimaginable happens. The mighty Forzak battleship rocks.

"What the fuck was that!?" Atany demands.

"Scanning," Sacar says.

"Checking," Daniel replies in unison with Sacar. Three seconds pass.

"Three warships, one thousand kilometers aft." Sacar says.

"Blast those fuckers," She orders. "What about the two in front?"

"They're gone," Daniel says. "They concentrated their attack on the same spot the other ship damaged."

"Roeton, call Benjamin and have him send a couple of his people to physically check the damage." She orders. "Continue firing until those ships are gone."

"Three ships destroyed." Sacar says after about twenty seconds.

"Status of the surface assault," Atany asks.

"Two more orbits and all our targets will be history," Sacar informs her.

"Continue assault," She commands.

"Captain, Benjamin on channel one." Roeton interrupts.

"Up's up, Commander? How's my ship?" Atany asks into her console.

"I'm at the impact site, Captain." His voice coming through the intercom. "The outer bulkhead covering half the span of the ship has been breached. It goes two decks up and about five meters into the drive section. The inner bulkheads are holding. I'll need a bit longer to determine the structural integrity of the upper assembly."

"Finish your inspection as soon as you can," She says. "Let me know when you're finished." She deactivates the intercom before he can answer. She focuses on the viewscreen, sitting silent.

The bombardment continues around the two orbits. Huge scars, kilometers wide, wrap around the planet. Explosions continue within the blasted areas, explosions visible from space.

"Captain, may I suggest we take the rest of the population into custody." Fental suggests.

"Custody?" She asks with an inquisitive look. "We can't do that. We don't have the manpower or logistics to handle an operation that big. I have a better idea. Hail the surface."

"I have the Horatha central command on the line." Roeton says after two minutes.

"On screen," Atany says. The image of Horath is now the leader of the battered species.

"Why have you attacked us?" He shouts at Atany, his voice heavy with sadness and anger.

"I am Dinema Atany of the starship Tartarus," The captain begins with a smile. "We have destroyed your military and industrial machines. We have sent your civilization back into the stone age. We are now in control."

"In control of what?" The Horathan leader asks in disbelief.

"Don't ask, just listen." Atany tells him. "The only thing you need to focus on is cleaning up the rubble left behind from the assault and getting things ready for our return. When we get back I will take my position as your leader. Failure to comply will result in the complete destruction of your species. Do you understand?"

"Understand what?" What are you talking about? Why?"

"Do you understand?" She shouts sternly.

"Yes," He answers, defeat showing in his eyes.

"Good," Atany replies. "Out." The screen goes back to showing Horath.

"Weapon's status?" She asks.

"All phaser banks power at ninety-three percent. Temperature in the green." Hoon reports.

"Photon torpedo compliment at ninety-seven percent." Sacar reports.

"Daniel, lifeform readings?" The captain asks.

"Sporadic readings, various size pockets everywhere," Daniel replies. "Negligible power readings around the globe."

"Let's leave them to clean up," Atany says. "We'll come back when we've completed our mission. The people on the surface are no longer a threat, at least not right now."

"Thank you, captain," Fental says softly. Atany nods, then continues,

"Helm, set course two, one, seven mark three, eight, eight. Stay at full impulse until further notice."

Chapter 8

"Captain's log, stardate 30401.21. As I expected, the conquest of the Horatha homeworld was easy, easier than I expected, actually. The only variable is the number of ships that are out of the system. We'll deal with them as we go. Now, off to our next rendezvous, Rill."

"Benjamin, report," She says into the mesh screen.

"Benjamin, here, Captain," His voice booms. "We'll be able to go to warp speed in about half an hour."

"Very good," Atany answers. "Let me know the minute you're finished."

"Will do, Captain. Out." The line goes silent.

"Tactical, status report." Atany asks.

"Scanners show all clear." Sacar reports. Hoon reports the same. The bridge crew takes a collective sigh of cautious relief. The battleship continues along its course uninterrupted. After forty minutes, Benjamin contacts the bridge with good news. The breaches are repaired enough to safely travel at warp speed.

"Warp five, Torres, now." Atany orders after speaking with Benjamin.

"Warp five, engaged." Torres says as the screen becomes a blur of streaking stars.

"ETA nine point five hours." Levi volunteers.

"Great, just in time for shift rotation." Fental complains. "You better get some rest." Atany says to Fental and Hawking. "You're going to need to be at your best." They agree and leave the bridge.

"I'm going to bed as well." Atany says with a smile. "I need to be at my best when we get there."

Thirty minutes later, as Fental lay in her bed trying to sleep, the door chime rings. She ignores the noise. The chime rings again several seconds later. She gets up and opens the door. Hawking is standing in the doorway.

"May I come in?" He asks. She steps back and motions him to enter without a word. He enters and the door whooshes closed.

"Are you upset about what Atany did?" He asks her cautiously.

"Of course I am," She snaps. "But I'm more upset at myself for not doing more to stop her."

"What could you have done?" He asks a bit stern. "Nothing," He answers for her. "And if you would have tried she would have probably had you thrown into an airlock and blasted you into space."

"You're probably right." She replies.

"I know I'm right. When the right time comes we'll know it. Until then we have to suck it up while we try to find supporters."

"What supporters? They're all on her side."

"Not all." He smiles slightly. "Remember, some are here against their wills, to some extent."

"Don't worry any more. Get some sleep." He tells her. "We'll be at Rill soon enough. You need to be at your best." He kisses her on the forehead. He looks down into her eyes for a moment. He leans in and gives her a long, hard kiss.

"Stay." She says.

"I can't." He answers. "I have some things to take care of. I'll be back to wake you in eight hours."

"Okay," She says with a smile as she pulls him in for another kiss. He leaves her quarters and she goes back to bed.

The doors to the drive section opens and Hawking enters the huge room. He walks several meters into the room and turns to the right. He studies the console for a few minutes without interruption.

"Is there something I can help you with, Commander?" Lieutenant Diana says, snapping him from his studies.

"No thanks." He answers. "I'm good for now." She smiles and walks away. After several more minutes of studying he turns his attention to the console to his left.

He moves down several more consoles down the line. He stops at the third one and studies it more in depth.

"Ah, here we go." He mumbles as he familiarizes himself with the controls. He inputs commands without anyone noticing. He continues for five minutes. He looks around when he is finished as sees no one.

The door chime rings. Fental squirms under her sheets. The door chime rings again. She gets out of bed. Hawking is standing in the doorway with a smile when it opens. She stands aside so he can enter and he does.

"We'll be at Rill in about an hour." He says as he enters. "Get dressed and we'll go grab some breakfast."

"Give me ten minutes and I'll be back." She tells him as she goes into the bathroom. She comes out in fifteen minutes, showered and dressed

"Let's go," She says and the two step into the hall. They get to the mess hall in minutes and get a light breakfast. Thirty minutes pass and the two leave the mess hall and head to the bridge. It takes less than a minute. They take their posts and look around the room. Noticeably absent are Atany and Daniel.

Atany and Daniel step off of the turbolift after fifteen minutes and take their seats. The night duty rotation enter the bridge and relieve the current personnel. Lieutenant Commander Aaron takes the secondary science station as Daniel had arrived at the post moments earlier.

"ETA ten minutes, Captain," Lieutenant Commander Merah tells the commanding officer after shift rotation is complete.

"Scanners showing two Rillian warships on an intercept course," Lieutenant Commander Korah, the tactical officer volunteers. "They'll be in weapons range in just under a minute."

"Okay, guys, lock all weapons on those ships and fire at will when they're in range." Atany orders with a smile. She sits back in her seat.

"So, how are you doing, Fental?" Dinema asks her first officer.

"Very well, Captain." She answers with a smile. "How are you?"

"I'm doing very well." The captain answers as she sits back in the big chair, focusing on the viewscreen with a smile. Fental looks at Hawking, who looks worried.

"Ships coming into range," Korah says. "Firing."

"Locking phasers," Lieutenant Commander Rigel says. "Firing." The two Rillian warships perform evasive maneuvers and suffer zero hits during the first volley. As the ships approach the Forzak battlecruiser, they evade two more volleys.

"Will you gentlemen please destroy those ships now." Atany asks sternly yet sarcastically.

"We are trying, Captain." Korah replies with similar sarcasm. "These little fuckers are nimble."

"Well, try a bit ha..." a rocking motion interrupts her train of thought.

"What was that?" She yells with frustration. "Daniel, damage?"

"Six Rillian warships aft!" Korah shouts with surprise.

"Ex vee pilots to your ships," She says into the intercom at the command station. She turns to look at Daniel, who is looking at her. She nods and, as he heads to the turbolift, she continues, "Archangels, report to the *Deliverance*. Off duty personnel report to stations." She deactivates the intercom.

Lieutenant Commander Rigel leaves her tactical position when Sacar replaces her. Lieutenants Borkin and Richards leave the helm as Levi arrives to replace them both. The other pilots and archangels converge on the ships in the hanger.

Seven minutes from the time Atany gave the order, the ex vee pilots and *Deliverance* crew are in their ships and the hanger deck doors are opening. The five ships drop from the *Tartarus'* belly and are greeted by phaser fire from the now seven Rillian warships, one being destroyed while the ships were launching.

The four fighters take up positions around the modified transport, one above, one below, one on the port and the other on the starboard. The five ships arc around and head straight for one of the warships not being fired at by Sacar and Korah.

The ships fire at the warship in unison as they slow down, concentrating more firepower in a confined area. Thirty seconds of continuous firing causes the Rillian warship to explode in a brilliant flash of matter and antimatter.

The five ships arc around as two more warships explode around them. The Forzak battlecruiser rocks several times as the group of small ships focus on the furthest of the four remaining warships. The group pulls the same maneuver and the warship explodes as the one to its left also explodes, being fired upon by the *Tartarus*.

The group rolls to the right, trying to get another ship in their sights. As the Rillian warship comes into the weapons range of the *Deliverance*, a bright flash from the right is followed by a violent rocking, causing the small transport to jolt to the left.

"Fuck!" Lieutenant Jasmine screams as she quickly moves her ex vee's control stick to the left. Her fighter cuts hard to the left, narrowly avoiding a collision with the transport.

The shockwave hits Lieutenant Commander Rigel's ex vee, which is above the now out-of-control *Deliverance*, sending her ship into a uncontrollable roll. Lieutenant Borkin, in the ex vee under the transport, is blinded from the flash of the explosion. His ex vee spins out of control, having also been hit by the shockwave.

As the pilots work to regain control of their ships, the *Tartarus* rocks once again, just as the two remaining Rillian warships explode under a barrage of weapons fire. The ships form up and arc around to the *Tartarus*.

"Hey, where's Ex Vee Two?" Borkin, in ex vee three, asks with some concern. "Jullian? Ex Vee Two? Where are you?"

"I'm not reading him on scanners." Lieutenant Hoon, on the *Deliverance*, says to the group.

"I don't see him anywhere." Lieutenant Jasmine tells them.

"The destruction of Ex Vee Two is what caused the shockwave that threw you out of control." Fental says.

"Come on home," Atany order with genuine solemn in her voice.

The four ships enter the hanger deck and the doors close under them. The crews disembark and leave the hanger deck with heads hung low, in silence. They make their way to the conference room and find Atany and Fental waiting. They enter and sit.

"We don't have a lot of time," Atany begins." So I'll make it short and sweet. I didn't know Jullian all that well, hell, I didn't know him at all. What I knew of him, he was a good guy. Wrong place, wrong time, shit out of luck."

"Before we could lock weapons, the Rillian ship got off the volley that took out Jullian." Fental adds. "If they hadn't hit Jullian it would have taken out the *Deliverance*."

"I know it sucks," Atany continues. "But I need you focused on what we are about to do. In five minutes we'll be engaging Rill itself. I need to know you're focused." She looks at each one while speaking.

"I can't speak for anyone else," Daniel begins. "But I'm ready to exact some revenge."

"So am I," Rigel agrees. Everyone else follows in agreement with the two. Atany stands and everyone else does likewise.

"Then let's teach these bug fuckers a lesson." Atany orders as she leaves the room with the rest of her crew behind her.

The captain and her entourage enter the bridge and see Rill on the viewscreen. They take their posts and settle in.

"Scanners clear, Captain," Korah informs her.

"We'll be in orbit in two point three minutes." Levi says next.

"Go to yellow alert." Atany orders and the klaxon sounds three times to inform the rest of the crew.

"We are being hailed by the central command." Reuben tells the captain. "By about twenty different divisions."

"Put me through to all of them." Atany commands calmly, with a smile.

"All set, Captain. You're on." Reuben says.

"People of Rill," She begins. "Your ambassador hired several saboteurs to ensure the failure of the mission we were sent on. When that didn't work, our return to this quadrant was met with a squadron of your warships. Your government's attempt failed. Now you pay. I wanted you to know why. Out." She signals Reuben to close the channel and he does.

"Tactical, fire all weapons. All military, all industrial and half of the population centers." Atany orders.

Both men acknowledge and comply. The main viewscreen now shows wave after wave of weapons fire raining down on the surface, huge scars and numerous explosions are seen in the wake of the assault.

Five orbits pass and a vast amount of the surface of Rill is laid waste. Fires rage out of control all over the planet.

• • •

"Are there any life signs below the surface?" Atany asks. Daniel scans for an entire orbit.

"There are seven subterranean complexes around the planet." He answers. "As we pass I'll relay geographical info to tactical so they can compute their firing solutions."

"You got that, Korah, Rigel?" The captain inquires.

"Yes, ma'am," Comes from both of them.

"Take out the first four," She orders

As they pass over each target, man and machine work in unison and, complex by complex, they destroy all the insectoid life on the planet. From the ship they see six phasers firing into the ground, penetrating deep into the dirt and rock, until they break into the caverns where each Rillian complex is.

Next is a volley of six torpedoes. The projectiles enter the holes made by the phasers and detonate within the caverns. After puffs of smoke rise from the holes, the ground within the blast areas collapse as the caverns bury those who survive the blasts.

"It takes ninety minutes to destroy all the underground complexes. Two orbits pass while the tactical and science stations complete their individual analysis.

"I'm detecting lifesigns everywhere, but not nearly as many as on Horath, Captain." Daniel reports.

"Confirming sporadic life signs," Korah and Rigel report in near unison.

"I also confirm sporadic lifeform readings." Hawking says with some sadness.

"Merah set a course for Chandar Two." Atany commands. "Richards, warp eight. Engage the invisibility shields."

"ETA Four hours," Merah tells her.

"No ships within scanner range." Korah volunteers.

"Put me on ship-wide intercom," Atany says after a few minutes.

"Ready, Captain," Reuben says.

"All hands, this is the captain," She begins. "All crewmembers meet in the hanger bay in five minutes." She stands and, as each of the bridge crew lock their consoles, they stand to join her.

When all the bridge crew are ready they enter the turbolift, in two different groups, for the ride to the lowest deck of the ship. The captain and her turbolift group reach the hanger deck along with Benjamin and the crew from the drive section. The entire crew is in the hanger deck in four minutes.

"I've called everyone here," Atany begins solemnly, "to pay homage to Lieutenant Jullian, who we lost earlier today. In honoring him we honor all of those we have lost since we first encountered B'Tong and began the ride that led us here." She weeps for several seconds and continues, "I didn't know him so I would like Lieutenant Commander Rigel to say a few words."

Rigel, pilot of Ex Vee One, comes before the crew. She lifts her head, which, after the events of the last few hours and the reduction of adrenaline now that the excitement is over, is hard to do, and takes a deep breath while looking around at her crewmates.

"I've known Jullian from the time we enlisted," She begins. "He had proven himself in several campaigns before entering the Ex Vee program. Since we've been assigned to this crew, Jullian proved himself a warrior in the defense of the Heaven and again on this last mission. Please bow your heads." She asks and all comply.

"Hear this, oh Gods of the multiverses, a warrior has entered your realm. Give him the honor and the glory bestowed upon the bravest of your creations. Give blessings to his bloodline that they may prosper and multiply to serve your wishes. In the names of the Gods we pray this offering. Amen." And "amen" is heard from the crew. They stand in bowed reverence for a moment. Hawking slips away.

Chapter 9

"Captain's log, stardate 30417.02. We are half an hour from Chandar Two. I am not anticipating any harder a time than we had on Rill. I pray to the gods that they suffer for the aggression they demonstrated towards us. If the gods allow, I will crush them out of existence."

"All stations, report." Atany orders.

"Orbit in twenty-four minutes," Lieutenant Commander Levi begins.

"Scanners reading all clear. No vessels in range." Lieutenant Commander Sacar says next.

"No energy abnormalities. No sub-space anomalies. No reading out of the ordinary." Daniel answers last.

Ten minutes pass. The silence on the bridge hangs thick in the air. The viewscreen shows Chandar Two in the center. Stars twinkling all around the brown, green and blue orb like diamonds in the moonlight.

● ● ●

"Scan the surface." Atany commands next. "I wanna know where they're hiding."

"Why do you think they're hiding?" Fental asks.

"We've already destroyed two planets, two races. I figure someone must have told them. Jacorrian perhaps," She explains.

"Logical. Very logical," Fental replies.

"I am unable to get any readings, Captain," Daniel says.

"Why the hell not?" Atany asks in disbelief.

"They are using some kind of invisibility shield." Daniel answers. "Similar to the Horatha's shield technology but I can't scan through it."

"How is that possible?" The captain asks the room.

"It seems the Chandrakan have been keeping some very good secrets." Hawking sarcastically comments.

"Keep a sharp eye, tactical," Atany says. "Since we can't scan the surface there may be ships we can't s…" As if on cue, the huge ship rocks side to side.

"Shit!" Atany says in disgust. "Fire full spread."

"There's nothing on my scanner, Captain," Sacar tells her. The ship rocks again.

"I know," She replies. "Set phasers for random firing sequences. Torpedoes set to widest possible dispersal pattern." The two men acknowledge their orders.

The Forzak battlecruiser begins to fire volley after volley, in every direction, randomly. Minutes go by as torpedo explosions blanket an area between five and seven kilometers away from the ship, the distance varying randomly as well.

"Ex Vee pilots to your fighters," Atany says into her intercom. Two minutes pass without any results. Then, on the viewscreen, in front of the Forzak ship, as several torpedoes explode, the silhouette of two Chandrakan warships appear in the light of the torpedo's afterglow. The ship rocks again.

"Target those ships and fire!" Atany shouts. The weapons fire from the *Tartarus* focuses on the two silhouettes and, after two volleys, both explode in brilliant bursts of light. As the two explosions fade a stream of plasma can be seen heading away from the coordinates of the ships that just blew up.

"Lock onto that plasma stream!" Atany shouts again. The phaser beams shoot out ahead of the plasma trail and, after several seconds, the phaser beams impact on the shields of the Chandrakan ship, blowing out their shield generators. In the screen, just becoming visible, is a four torpedo volley heading for the Forzak ship. They make impact on the forward shields, causing the lights to flicker. The two torpedoes that Sacar fired, following the phaser volley, rip through the hull and destroy the ship from the inside out. The *Tartarus* rocks again.

In six minutes the ex vee pilots report to the bridge that they are ready to go. The hanger deck doors open and the three ships drop from the belly of the beast.

"Three Chandrakan warships have been destroyed." Atany's voice sounds through the pilots' headsets. "There are an unknown number of ships left. Fly out ahead of the ship and try to draw fire. Try to get a count and take them out."

"Copy that, Captain," Rigel answers. "Follow me," She says to her fellow pilots as she kicks in her turbo thrusters and blasts ahead of the other two ships. In a second they follow suit. They kick in their turbo thrusters and fall into formation. A brief moment of quietness allows the three ships to fly ahead of the forward blast areas. As the fighters bank around they see the *Tartarus* as she fires all weapons aft. The explosions remind Rigel of the fireworks displays at the Armistice Day celebration on Orancara Four. The forward bombardment continues once the small fighters clear the area.

"What does Alliance intelligence have on the Chandrakan scientific progress?" Atany asks. Both Daniel and Hawking jump on the task. It takes nearly two minutes.

"There is nothing in the Alliance database about their invisibility shield technology." Daniel tells her. "There are rumors about a rogue scientist, a Doctor T'Pol"A, who is reportedly working on such technology. There is nothing about his progress."

"My sources inform me that T'Pol'A has, in fact, completed the shield research and, as we can see, they are right." Hawking says next. "They also have complete technical information about the generators themselves."

"What must we do to obtain that information?" Atany asks.

"They want schematics on the Forzak weapons systems." He answers. She thinks for a long few seconds, her mind racing in devious ways.

"Can we give them incomplete schematics that will fool an engineer?"

"You forget, Captain," Hawking answers her. "I'm a computer genius. Give me an hour and I'll modify the file in a way only I can detect."

"That's pretty cocky," Daniel says.

"Yes it is," Hawking retorts. "And that's only because I can do what I say I can do."

"Awesome," Daniel says with a smile. "Can't wait to see the finished product."

"Do it," Atany tells him. He spins to his console and gets to work.

The ship rocks, causing several consoles on the bridge to short out.

"Ex Vee One, Ex Vee Four, I got em," Lieutenant Jasmine says over her fighter's communications array. "Follow me in." The three fighters, in a triangle formation, swing around. Jasmine fires and her weapons hit the shield of the Chandrakan warship.

"Got em," Rigel and Borkin say simultaneously. All three ships continue to fire continuously.

"Lock on to where they are firing at." Atany orders. "Help the Ex Vees blast those fuckers." Several volleys from the *Tartarus* along with the fighter's firepower overwhelm the Chandrakan defensive systems and the ship explodes in a brilliant matter/antimatter explosion.

The three fighters fly through the explosion, avoiding leftover debris and continue orbiting the Forzak battlecruiser at twenty kilometers distance while the blanket of weapons fire detonates midway between the big ship and tiny fighters.

The fighters search for Chandrakan warship silhouettes. Ten minutes pass with no further signs of the enemy ships. Another ten minutes pass.

"Roeton, bring the Ex Vees back on board." Atany tells her communications officer.

"Yes, ma'am," He answers as he manipulates the controls. He passes along the captain's orders and the fighters return to the ship.

"Helm, ETA to Orancara Four at warp five?" Atany inquires.

"One point two hours." He answers.

"As soon as the hanger doors are secure do it," She says. "Ari, tell your contacts to meet us at Orancara Four, on the dark side of the moon, in one point two hours." Both men comply. Ari continues with the schematic modifications.

The battlecruiser enters orbit right on time. There is only one other ship in orbit and it has no transponder signal.

"Ari, would you hail that ship, please," Atany orders with a smile.

"No problem," He says. He hails them and the viewscreen changes to show the shadowed silhouette of a humanoid.

"Greetings, Captain," The shadow says with an electronically distorted voice. "Greetings, Professor. Do you have what we discussed?"

"He does," Atany interrupts. "But you will deal with me. We can do this one of two ways. First, you beam over here with the merchandise and we do our business here, or, a simultaneous data transfer."

"I'm sure you know I will agree with a simultaneous data transfer." The shadowed figure answers. "We must also agree to remain until the schematics have been verified."

"I would expect nothing more," Atany smiles while replying.

"Then let us do this," He says.

The captain looks over at Daniel, who acknowledges the start of the data transfer. She signals Hawking, who begins the download of the Forzak phaser systems. It takes eight minutes for the downloads to complete, due to the alien ship's inadequate computer system.

Hawking reviews the data file and, after fifteen minutes, acknowledges its authenticity. It takes the engineer on the alien ship a bit longer and finally acknowledges the same. The two commanders resume visual communication.

"Are you satisfied?" Atany asks the shadowed figure.

"My engineer says the schematics are good, very good." The alien captain answers. "I believe our business is concluded."

"Very good," Atany replies. "Good health and happiness to you." She smiles as Roeton closes the channel.

On the viewscreen the alien ship turns and flies away slowly.

"Sacar," Atany says, still looking at the screen. From the side of the screen two torpedoes come into view, heading toward the alien craft. The first one impacts the shields right above the main engines, destroying the shield generators. The second penetrates the outer bulkhead and detonates inside of the engine room. The ship instantly vaporizes.

"Why the fuck did you do that!?" Hawking shouts in shock and anger.

"What's your problem, Ari?" Atany asks with genuine surprise.

"They were my friends!" He answers. "The schematics were no good! There was no reason to kill them!"

"Look, Ari," She starts with a smile. "Eventually we would have had to destroy them. I took care of the problem proactively." Giggles come from most of the other bridge crew. Hawking gets up and storms off the bridge, anger pronounced in his facial expressions.

"Helm, lay in a course back to Chandar Two, full impulse. Engage the invisibility shields." The captain commands. The massive battleship cruises along, unseen by anything passing by, heading to fulfill the destiny of the Chandrakan race.

Forty-five minutes later Hawking comes back onto the bridge, walking straight to the captain's chair. He takes a breath.

"My apologies, Captain." He begins. His pride, arrogance and intellect are keeping him strong. "Though I don't agree with what you did, I should not have freaked out on you the way I did. The captain is, was, my friend. Even now you can still surprise me." He smiles at her.

"No worries, Ari," A huge smile spreads across her face. "I knew you'd be back. How about looking over the schematics and find a weakness we can exploit." He looks over at Fental and his smile widens as she smiles back at him.

"I'm on it," Hawking answers the captain as he heads back to his station.

"Oh, Ari," Atany continues." How long will you need?"

"Give me a couple of hours or so," He replies.

"Excellent," She says. "Helm, increase speed to warp two point five."

"ETA two point seven hours." Levi tells her.

"You have more than enough time, Commander." She says smiling.

Two hours pass quietly as the ship makes its way through the blackness of space.

"Captain," Daniel interrupts. "I've got three Chandrakan warships at the very edge of long range sensors. Distance four point nine, two light years."

"Helm, alter course and bring us just within their sensor range. Once there, deactivate the invisibility shields. When they see us, return course to Chandar Two then reactivate the invisibility shields." Atany says.

The ship veers to the left. It takes just over a minute to get within the Chandrakan sensors.

"The ships have changed course, Captain," Daniel says. "They are on an intercept course."

"Helm," Atany says.

The big ship veers to the right and, in seconds, is back on its previous course. After a minute the ship disappears, continuing its trip. The Forzak battlecruiser easily advances ahead of the three ships.

"The Chandraka are in pursuit," Daniel tells the captain. "They are at warp five."

"Maintain course and speed," Atany orders. "Allow them to pass by us. Use evasive maneuvers if necessary."

It takes three minutes for the Chandrakan warships to catch up to the larger battlecruiser. The huge ship glides to the right, enough to allow the three smaller ships to pass. Once they pass, the *Tartarus* lazily returns to its original course.

"Captain, I think I found what we need," Hawking says with some excitement in his voice. She gets up and goes to his station, followed by Fental and Daniel. The three gather around the seated scientist.

"Their system is a two component setup," Hawking starts. "The weakness is the connector conduit. It is rated at five hundred terawatts squared."

"You call that a weakness?" Fental asks. "That's a shitload of power."

"The field output is square to the fifth power of that, so, yeah, that's the weakness."

"Point taken," She replies.

"How can we exploit that?" The captain asks.

"We have to bombard one specific point with enough energy that the conduit overloads." He explains.

"How much energy are you talking?" She asks.

"I'm talking in the magnitude of sixty-two billion, five hundred million terawatts." He answers.

"Nothing can produce that much power," Fental says somewhat astonished.

"This ship can," Hawking interjects. "In a manner of speaking."

"Explain," Atany says.

With the combined arsenal of this ship and the *Deliverance*, we could generate the necessary energy." He answers. "I'll have the firing solutions computed by the time we arrive."

"When will that be?" Atany focuses her attention to the helmsmen.

"ETA thirty minutes." Levi tells them.

"That's how long you have." Atany tells Hawking.

"Ah, plenty of time," He says as he turns his head and focuses on the task at hand, oblivious to all things. Atany, Fental and Daniel return to their stations and continue the mission.

"I've got the best firing solutions ready and programmed," Hawking says. "Need a minute to program the computer on the *Deliverance*."

"Great," Atany replies. "Helm, warp eight, now."

"ETA forty-five seconds," Levi says after a few seconds.

"Daniel, get your archangels and get your ship ready for launch." Atany orders.

"You'll need the Ex Vees as well, Captain." Hawking adds.

"Ex Vees, prepare for launch, on the double." Atany says inter her communications panel.

The *Tartarus* comes out of warp speed on the outer fringes of the Chandrakan system. Heading at full impulse, it takes the ship two minutes to reach Chandar Two. By the time the battlecruiser achieves orbit it is accompanied by the small, modified transport and the three smaller fighters.

"The biggest issue," Hawking begins. "Is to keep any ship trying to stop us, away. Both we and the *Deliverance* need to maintain continuous firing for twelve point five minutes. The fighters need to protect us."

"We have aft weapons," Atany reminds him.

"Yes," Hawking agrees. "The *Deliverance*, however, does not. We will also be using the aft torpedoes in the assault, so only aft phasers can be used for defense."

"Sacar, you monitor the assault weapons," Atany starts. "Lieutenant Commander Korah, keep a sharp eye aft and be ready on those damn phasers." Both men acknowledge her orders.

"Fire on my mark," Atany says calmly, deliberately. "And… mark."

The massive battlecruiser begins firing all its forward weapons at the same time as the tiny modified transport. The three fighters fly in a circular pattern around the attacking ships. The bombardment continues uninterrupted for over ten minutes.

By the eleventh minute the shield starts to flicker, exposing a section of the city below, naked and defenseless. As the timer rounds eleven and a half minutes the aft phasers fire. The fighter pilots see the silhouette of the warship when the phaser beams hit the cloaked ship.

The fighters form up and start their attack run. As their weapons fire assault the shields of the Chandrakan ship, the Forzak phasers cut into the hull. Decompression explosions rip through the ship, deck by deck. As the ship explodes, debris bounces off of another concealed vessel, overloading a few of its shield generators.

The Ex Vees arc around and lock onto the ship flickering in and out of view. They fire simultaneously and in unison with the *Tartarus*. This warship, like the other, exploded after a few seconds of assault.

The fighters continue circling and, as Rigel looks down at the impact point, she sees the explosion of the shield generator conduit overload and a section of the shield grid collapses.

"Deliverance, Ex Vees, begin a low level assault on the other shield generators." Atany's voice sounds through the ship's radio. They confirm their orders and head into the planet's atmosphere. Swinging into formation, they shoot down, seeing nothing but clouds below. As they orbit around the planet, a hole in the clouds appears and the actual surface of the planet is revealed.

The ships level off at twenty-five meters above the surface. As they search out the shield generators, they take pop-shots at the Chandrakans running for cover. It takes just over a minute for the assault squad to find the next generator. The conduit is destroyed after a short, multi-vessel barrage.

The second shield drops and more of the city beneath comes into view. From the viewscreen the bridge crew see the allied ships flying off to right, leaving the region under the first shield unobstructed.

"Fire all our weapons at the military and industrial structures on the surface but leave the civilians alone." Atany orders. "As more shields drop, blast the structures that become visible. Korah, as you fire, keep watching for any other ships entering the system."

It takes another three minutes for the next shield to go down. As the shields drop, the weapons fire coming from orbit obliterates the targets on the surface. Bodies fly as torpedoes blast into factories. Large strips of buildings, vegetation, vehicles and living beings are vaporized by the intense heat of the five meter diameter phaser beams, all six of them.

Five hours of relentless assault sees the last of the shield generators blowing up and, thirty minutes later, the last of the surface structures explodes in a ball of bright orange, red and yellow flame.

"There is one stronghold underground, Captain," Daniel tells Atany. "It is a huge structure. Hundreds of rooms of various sizes with mazes of corridors. The center chamber is on the bottom,

• • •

eleven levels deep. I'm getting unusual reading from within that chamber."

"Explain your definition of 'unusual'." Atany asks.

"I'm reading thousands of bioelectrical impulses. Hundreds of thousands of impulses." Daniel explains.

"Living beings?"

"Yes, Captain."

"A nursery?"

"These readings suggest that each individual impulse is co-cooned."

"What?" Atany's face distorted with inquisition.

"They're eggs, Captain,"

"A hatchery," Atany says with more confidence.

"That's my thought," He replies.

"Ex Vees, return to the Tartarus," Roeton's voice tells the pilots.

"Where on our way," Rigel radios back. The fighters climb and, just as they are about to exit the atmosphere, out of the sun, a warship becomes visible. Ex Vee Three is hit by the energy bolts fired by the now visible ship and explodes in a brilliant explosion, creating a shockwave that sends the two remaining fighters spinning out of control.

Rigel and Jasmine regain control of their ships after about two minutes and form up side by side. The Chandrakan ship breaks through the clouds and is greeted by the two fighters. The women bring their ships over the top of the warship and, from behind, un-load their combined arsenal along the spine of the vessel.

As the fighters complete their run and fly out in front of the warship, the shield generators short out, leaving the ship vulnerable. The ship is still intact. Both women stare at each other through their canopy glass, worry showing on both of their faces. They know the worried look is because they are now in the sights of the Chandrakan tactical officer.

They signal each other to break off in different directions. Just as they implement their plan, the warship explodes with a thunderous boom. The women arc their ships from different directions and see the *Deliverance* flying through the flaming debris.

"Thanks for the assist, *Deliverance*," Rigel says.

"Our pleasure," Daniel answers.

"Yeah, thanks," Jasmine adds.

"Let's get back to the *Tartarus*," Rigel suggests.

"Ex Vee One and Ex Vee Two, return to the ship." Atany says, as if to read Rigel's mind. "*Deliverance*, there is a structure under the surface of the planet. We are sending you all the data we have. The attack has to be a ground assault. There are no life signs within a ten kilometer diameter around your landing coordinates but be careful none the less."

The transport sets down behind the ruins of huge building, hoping to avoid any electronic defensive systems that may still be active. The archangels are prepping for their new mission… enter the underground complex and destroy the hatchery.

The door of the transport opens and the six archangels disembark. Daniel exits to the right, followed by his helmsman, Lieutenant Torres and his engineer, Lieutenant Voltarus. Lieutenant Commander Nire, the medic, exits to the left with Lieutenant Hoon, the tactical officer and Lieutenant Richards, the demolitions expert.

The two groups are walking the one point six kilometers to the entrance of the underground complex. The six are wearing the latest in Alliance combat gear. The helmet, breast and back plates and arm and leg protectors are made of a deuterium allow wired with a series of micro-capacitors. The capacitors absorb the power from directed energy weapons, protecting the wearer from the deadly discharge.

The electronic aspect of the gear is the communications array. It has the microphone and speaker tied in so the channel stays open for simultaneous communications between all six soldiers. A transparent piece of plastic covering one eye completes the electronic portion of their equipment. This plastic piece displays status information to the soldier, such as life signs, communications signal strength, and terrain display with enemy troop locations.

Each soldier has, as a sidearm, the EX-1911 multi-barrel combat pistol, capable of firing both barrels in unison or out of sync, depending on the situation. The main weapon each archangel has is the newest, most technologically advanced weapon, the MX-1903 assault phaser rifle. The only soldiers in the Alliance that have these rifles are the six archangels readying to leave the transport.

They make their way down the rubble strewn street, carefully eyeing the terrain around them. There is no sign of life anywhere in sight. They turn left four blocks from the transport and cautiously watch ahead for movement.

They make their way half a kilometer when movement ahead stops them in their tracks. The teams take cover amongst the rubble littering the sides of the street.

From around a corner half a block ahead a motorized, mechanized combat drone appears. It stands two meters tall with three large tires mounted on hydraulic pistons on each side. The main body is a plain rectangular box. On top is a turret with eight barrels, covering all directions. A small antennae array sits atop the turret.

As the archangels watch motionless, a slight breeze pushes a large piece of wrinkled paper into the road. The drone stops, spins its turret and incinerates the paper, in the blink of an eye. The automaton spins its turret one last time, scanning the area for any further movement.

The drone rolls across the street and heads away from the group. The two teams continue to make their way silently down the long, straight road. It takes the teams fifteen minutes to get into a position to observe the entrance of the complex.

From their vantage point the teams can see a huge metallic door, ten meters square, covering the entrance within a massive concrete bunker built into the side of a manufactured mound, topped with the remnants of a solar farm. On each side of the door are two laser turrets built into the walls.

"Richards, Voltarus, get ready to advance on and blow that door." Daniel says. "Nire, take the upper right. Torres, lower right. Hoon, lower left. Fire on my mark. After we take out the turrets we'll cover Richards and Voltarus." Everyone acknowledges and take up positions to take out the lasers.

Richards and Voltarus make their way ahead of the other four, who are prone in the rubble. They reach the end of protection.

"We're in position," Richards says softly into his headset.

"Copy that," Daniel says. "Fire." The four fire their phaser rifles, each at their designated targets. As the phaser beams hit the laser turrets, Richards and Voltarus run toward the metallic door, explosives in hand.

As the two soldiers reach the opposite side of the street, the four turrets explode in fireballs, raining small chunks of concrete on the two men. They reach the door and put tiny matter/anti-matter packets on each side, as high as they can reach. Once they finished, they laid more along the bottom, for the entire span of the door. They run back to their hiding spot without incident.

The two make their way back to their teams and, once there, Daniel detonates the ordnance. The explosion deafens the archangels as debris flies around them. The ground shakes for several seconds as smoke and dust roll over the hidden soldiers, who remain motionless.

Fifteen seconds pass and the first drone comes rolling down the street from the left, coming to investigate the explosion. Two heartbeats later another comes rolling from the right, followed almost immediately by one from behind the teams. The three drones converge at the now destroyed entrance.

"Ready up, archangels," Daniel says softly. "Richards, Voltarus, take the one on the left. Torres, Hoon, the one on the right. Nire, you and I are on the center." All acknowledge when they have their targets in their sights. "Fire," Daniel orders.

The six beams converge on the three targets. The drones are unable to determine where the attack is coming from due to multiple, simultaneous hits. It takes about four seconds of continuous fire before the first one explodes, followed quickly by the other two.

The six soldiers remain motionless for another two minutes, making sure the destruction of the drones doesn't attract more. When Daniel is confident they are safe, he cautiously stands, followed by the other five.

As they cross the deserted street, they break into their two teams. They widen the gap between them as they go, approaching the door from both sides and out of the line of fire from anything inside.

Daniel stands on the right side with his team and Nire is on the left with hers. Daniel kneels as he looks inside the huge corridor, looking for any sign of defense. He turns back out of sight and Nire looks in, staying upright. There is nothing but quiet and stillness.

The two teams enter simultaneously, hugging the walls as they move in cautiously. Fifty meters in the corridor comes to an end at a perpendicular corridor.

"Okay," Daniel says. "You go left, we'll go right."

"Good luck," Nire says.

"You too. Maintain contact and be careful," Daniel finishes as he and his team head down the corridor. It takes about thirty seconds for the two teams to loose visual contact with each other. No one notices that the corridors gently curve inward.

"They just separated at the end of the entry corridor," Fental, at the science station in Daniel's absence, tells the captain.

"The area around the *Deliverance* is clear of lifeforms." Sacar says.

"The area around us is still clear," Korah says last.

"Excellent," Atany says. "Keep them in your sights, Fental."

"Don't worry, Captain," Fental assures her. "I've got em."

The corridor ends at a door two hundred meters in. On the wall to the left is a small square with a round button in the middle. Daniel presses the button, which glows green when pushed.

The door opens after nearly five seconds. The team discovers it is a lift. They get in and the door closes. On the wall to the right of the door is a rectangle with three vertical buttons.

"I thought the scans showed eleven levels?" Torres asks.

"They did," Daniel replies.

"So much for a direct route," Voltarus says.

"I hope the other team is having better luck," Daniel says as he presses the bottom button.

Nire and her team encounter a door at the end of their corridor one hundred and fifty meters in. The control panel on the wall is a horizontal rectangle. Within the rectangle are four round buttons. On each button is a symbol.

"What the hell?" Nire says inquisitively. Hoon scans the panel with his tricorder. It takes nearly thirty seconds.

"It's a key pad for the door." He says.

"Thanks, Lieutenant Obvious," She responds with a smile. "What's the fucking code?" Hoon punches in the code and the door opens, revealing a steep stairway going several stories then disappearing into the looming darkness.

"Great," Nire says. "Could've been a turbolift, at least. Let's get going." She finishes as she heads down the stairs, the rest of her team following.

The lift stops at the third level and the door opens. The three step out of the lift and are standing in a room fifty meters square. Rows of tables with chairs on both sides fill the room. At the far end of the room are three evenly spaced corridors going into the unknown.

"A mess hall?" Torres half-asks.

"I think so," Daniel answers. The three start walking around the room, up and down the rows of tables, looking for any information about the complex. They find nothing.

"Which way, boss?" Voltarus asks Daniel.

"Coincidentally there are three corridors and three of us." Daniel answers. "Take your pick." Voltarus heads to the one on the right while Torres heads down the left side. Daniel goes down the center corridor.

As they reach the bottom of the stairs, Nire and the team see the main corridor heading straight into darkness. Ten meters from the stairs is an intersection. The intersecting corridor, like the one in front, goes straight into darkness in both directions.

"Where do we go now?" Richards asks.

"You go that way," She tells him, pointing to the right corridor. "Hoon, you go that way," She points to the left corridor. She heads down the center.

"Report," Atany orders.

"All six archangels are exploring alone," Fental replies. "In six thousand meters most of the crewmen will be reunited. We just can't tell what's lying in wait."

"Well, we'll do what we can to minimize their risks, but their training will allow them to prevail." Atany says.

"I hope you're right," Fental replies.

"So do I," Atany adds.

"Captain," Fental says with confused panic. "I'm picking up Chandrakan life signs. Maybe a dozen but they have to have some kind of dampening field. I can't pinpoint their locations."

"Let the archangels know." The captain tells Roeton.

"I can't get through," Roeton reports. There is a jamming device preventing direct communication.

"So, we just get to watch," Atany says to no one in particular.

Daniel walks down the hall, passing door after door. He checks each door as he passes and finds nothing but crew quarters, each being a five by ten meter room with two bunks and two lockers on one side of the room and a desk with two chairs against the opposite wall. The back three meters of the room consists of a shower, sink and toilet with a partial wall separating it from the front part. Every room, on both sides, has the identical layout.

After what seems to be a thousand meters, he comes to an intersection. To the left and right, the corridors extend just over twenty meters then turn to head back in the direction he just came. In front of him, five meters beyond the intersection is a door with a control panel similar to the one he encountered three levels up.

As he inspects the control panel he pushes the button. The button lights up. While waiting for the lift, or what he believes is a lift, Torres and Voltarus join him, coming from the adjacent corridors.

"What did you find?" He asks them.

"Nothing but crew quarters." Torres answers, as does Voltarus.

"That's all I found as well," Daniel tells them. The door opens and, much to Daniel's relief, it's a lift. The three get on and when the door closes they notice four buttons on the control panel. He pushes the bottom button and the lift starts to move as the button lights up.

Nire sees the first door some fifty meters down the center corridor. She enters to find tables covered in laboratory equipment, some she recognizes and other pieces leave her clueless. She pulls a small visual recorder from her equipment belt and starts filming the equipment she doesn't recognize. After five minutes she leaves the room, heading down the hall.

She enters the next room and finds the same thing, more unknown equipment mixed with the type of lab equipment she uses all

the time. Nire takes several small handheld devices she did not recognize and puts them in her pocket with the hope of figuring out
what they do when she is back on the *Tartarus*.

She moves through all the rooms in the corridor and finds
the same. At the end of the corridor is a set of stairs. She goes down.
She enters a large room with rows of chairs facing the far wall,
which has two large video monitors on it. In between the monitors
is a door. It reminds her of an auditorium.

She makes her way to the door and opens it. The door opens
into a room ten meters long by eight meters wide. There is a desk
and chair at the left side of the room facing her. The wall behind the
desk is covered in shelves filled with books, as is the right wall.
There is a door in the wall directly across from her. She looks around
for a moment then goes to the desk. She sits and starts rifling through
the papers in front of her, hoping to get some insight into the Chandraka.

The door of the turbolift opens and the three men step out
into a small lobby with corridors at the far end heading left and right.
As the three step further into the lobby Daniel notices shadows on
the walls of both corridors. He lifts his hand and makes a fist as he
stops. Torres and Voltarus stop in place, freezing like statues.

Daniel gestures to the shadows. When the two men see them
they draw their assault phasers and look at Daniel. He motions
Torres to the left wall and Voltarus to the right one. The men put
their backs to the walls and slide down to one knee, taking aim at
the opposite corridors. Daniel lies on the floor aiming at the wall in
front of him.

Torres counts four shadows coming down the right corridor.
Voltarus counts five from the left. One at a time the shadows become
Chandrakan soldiers. Seven of them are in the lobby when the lead
soldier sees Daniel on the floor. The reptile has no time to react.

"Fire!" Daniel shouts and the three men begin a simultaneous barrage of phaser fire. None of the Chandrakan soldiers have

time to draw their weapons before each one is cut to pieces by the steady flow of high energy plasma. In less than two minutes all nine Chandrakan are on the floor with their internal organs beside them.

When the battle is over the three ex-Alliance officers stand up and cautiously make their way to investigate the carnage. The faint sound of running shoes is starting to get louder. The three officers wait for several seconds, trying to determine the direction of the footsteps.

They realize that the sounds are coming from the left corridor and assume a tactical position. Daniel is in the center of the corridor on one knee. Torres is standing to his left and Voltarus to the right. The sound gets louder, echoing in the darkness.

The shadowy image of running figure starts to emerge from the darkness. The Alliance officers stiffen their posture, waiting for a clear shot.

The footsteps get louder and, out of the darkness, Lieutenant Richards, running at full stride, suddenly stops.

"Hey! Hey! Hey!" Richards shouts in fear when he sees the three rifles pointing at him. "What the fuck!"

"Why are you running into a combat area?" Daniel asks sternly.

"I heard weapons fire," Richards explains. "Came to check it out."

"Why run in blindly?" Daniel continues.

"When the firing stopped, I figured you had it under control."

"Where are Nire and Hoon?" Torres asks.

"We came to an intersection," Richards begins. "We each went down different corridors. That was about forty minutes ago. All I found was offices and labs. When I heard your phaser fire I came running."

"Okay," Daniel says after several seconds. "Richards, you and Torres go back and see if you can reconnect with Nire and Hoon.

Voltarus and I will go this way." He points to the corridor on the right. The men acknowledge and head off.

Nire, lost in the reports on the desk, doesn't hear the door to her left open. About half way open the hinges squeak. Nire slides off the chair, dropping to one knee, and aims her sidearm at the door. The door swings fully open as the wall behind Hoon's head explodes.

"Hey!" Hoon screams in fear. "What are you doing?"

"Sorry," Nire says apologetically. "Didn't hear you come in."

"So you thought what? I was Chandrakan?"

"I didn't know. That's the point." She says. "You shouldn't bitch. At least you're not dead."

"Why so jumpy?" Hoon asks.

"I've been looking over some of the paperwork on the desk." She starts. "I'm not fluent in Chandrakan but I think what I'm reading can have serious implications. We need to find Daniel." The two leave the office, heading down the unknown corridor.

It takes nearly ten minutes before Nire and Hoon meet up with Richards and Torres, who immediately notices the worry on her face.

"What's wrong, Nire?" Torres asks.

"I need to speak to Daniel, now." She says with some panic. "Where is he?"

"He and Voltarus went in the other direction."

"We need to find him now."

"We'll have to run." Torres replies.

"So be it," Nire says as she starts to run, the other three following.

Daniel and Voltarus follow the corridor one hundred, fifty meters. They turn left and continue twenty meters to a door on the left at the end of the corridor. The door opens with the push of a button. The two enter cautiously.

The room is about fifty meters wide by three hundred meters long. There are five, ninety meter long, rows of machines on each side of the room from beginning to end. In the center of the room are two rows of tables, all filled with a wide array of sophisticated equipment. At the center of the far wall is a double door.

Each row is made up of ninety-five machines. Each machine is three meters long by one meter wide. There is a one meter square glass box on each side of the machine and the center square meter houses the control panel. The only exceptions are the rows against the wall. These units are positioned so the control panel is a half a meter away from the wall and the single glass box is open to the isle. In all there are nine hundred and fifty units with a total of one thousand, seven hundred and ten glass boxes.

"What do you think they did in here?" Voltarus asks.

"I have no idea," Daniel answers. "I know what some of this stuff is for but most of it is beyond me." They walk slowly past the tables, trying to figure out what the Chandraka were doing in that room.

They are about two thirds of the way down the row when the door opens and the other four archangels enter the room.

"What's going on?" Daniel asks the four.

"I found some documents in an office," Nire begins as the group walks to the two men. "It appears that this complex is a breeding farm."

"A what?" Daniel asks.

"This is where the Chandrakan continue their species." She explains. "The female's eggs are collected, inseminated, and incubated in this very room."

"When we got here these machines were all empty." Torres tells her.

"This is a bad thing," She replies.

"Why is this a bad thing?" Daniel asks.

• • •

"Because this means that all the eggs are in the final stages of development. According to the documents there are about two point five million eggs ready to hatch."

"Where are they?" Voltarus asks with nervousness lingering in his voice.

"They've got to be on the lowest level." Nire says.

Daniel and Torres turn and look at the double doors at the end of the room. The other four look in the same direction and, only now, see the doors.

"Do you think?" Daniel asks Nire.

"It's the only way I see." She answers. The six walk toward the doors.

The turbolift travels slower than the others. Along with the final level being deeper than the other levels, the ride seems to take hours instead of minutes.

The doors open to a room five times larger than the one they just left. There are rows and rows of units similar to the ones above. These rows are stacked ten high. The six enter the room and look around in astonishment, no one speaking.

"How are we going to destroy all of these eggs?" Richards asks.

"More importantly, what happens when we try?" Daniel asks.

"What do you mean?" Hoon asks.

"Since we've been in here we haven't encountered any electronic defenses, only the nine soldiers a few levels back." Daniel tells them. "With the importance of this place, we should have encountered some kind of electronic countermeasures."

"Let's deal with one thing at a time," Voltarus suggests. "Let's wipe out these eggs before they hatch, then we can worry about getting out."

"Before we blow this place, let's look around and see what else is in this chamber." Daniel orders. The five acknowledge and start slowly moving through the huge room.

• • •

As the group moves cautiously toward the far end of the room they search every orifice along the way. Progress is slow yet methodical. They get to the other end of the room and find a single, large door near the right corner. The six make a circle in front of it.

"Any suggestions on how to destroy this room?" Daniel asks.

"Only one way I see," Torres replies. "Destroy the control panels right down the line."

"That'll take some time," Hoon responds.

"We can seal this chamber so when they hatch they can't get out and die off. It'll take less time." Voltarus adds. There is silence for several minutes as Daniel considers the available options.

"Okay," Daniel begins. "We're doing both." Confusion appears on everyone's faces. "We're going to seal the turbolift we came down in. On our way back here we are going to destroy as many of the egg chambers as we can. We'll take this lift out then collapse the shaft from the top." All acknowledge and the group make their way back to the other end of the room.

Hoon presses the button on the wall and the turbolift doors open. Richards enters the lift. He raises his phaser rifle and cuts a large hole in the ceiling. After side-stepping the falling metal he sets his rifle to full power. He aims at the top of the shaft and fires, working the beam side by side as he brings it down.

After several long seconds of fire, chunks of rock and metal came crashing down onto the bottom of the shaft, nearly crushing Richards. When the rubble finishes falling, the young lieutenant aims his rifle through an opening near the top of the entry and fires at the opposite wall of the shaft. The shaft wall explodes and tons more rubble fall on top of what is already down, successfully sealing the room from that end.

"Look around for any other doors, stairways or other rooms at this end." Daniel commands. Everyone looks around and, after about five minutes, all agree this part of the job is complete.

• • •

"Everyone pick a row and let's start destroying these machines." Daniel orders next. Each member of the team pick their rows, leaving several open in between each person. They step in a few meters and turn around.

"Fire at will," Daniel shouts and all six fire simultaneously at the units at the beginning of the row. They walk backwards slowly as they continue to fire. Explosions blast through the machines, shattering the glass boxes. Eggs fall to the floor, cracking open when they hit.

It takes nearly ten minutes for the archangels to reach the door at the far wall. Explosions continue to rock the rows of machines as electrical fires spread wildly throughout the room. The temperature in the room climbs by ten degrees as the smell of death starts to creep in.

"Get on the lift," Daniel tells the team when the door opens. The archangels get on the turbolift, fitting in tightly. The lift goes up to the level above and the door opens. The six exit the lift, Richards being last. He blocks the closing of the door with his foot as he aims his rifle at the floor of the lift. Here he cuts a huge square, nearly the entire surface of the floor and as the metal plate falls down the shaft Richards fires at the shaft walls.

Tons of rubble fall into the bottom of the shaft as Richards continues firing into the concrete walls. He continues firing for just over a minute as his beam is now above his head and the rubble is very nearly floor level.

The team makes their way through the large room, heading back to the corridor. They enter the corridor and steadily yet cautiously return in the direction they came. As they approach the lobby, the team avoids the corpses of the nine Chandrakan soldiers.

Heading back through the lobby, the six climb aboard the turbolift at the end. The door closes and the lift heads up four decks. The door opens and the team exits the lift two by two, walking very near the walls of the corridor.

As they approach the intersection of the corridor, a noise ahead makes them stop. Daniel sees the familiar shadows heading down the left and right corridors. He lies down on the floor near the wall and Nire, walking along the opposite wall, does the same. Torres drops to one knee behind Daniel. Richards does the same behind Nire while Voltarus and Hoon stand tall.

The team makes out six distinct shadows in each corridor. As the Chandrakan soldiers appear in the corridor their attention is focused on each other rather than the corridor. Eight soldiers make it into the corridor's intersection before they see the six archangels.

Daniel sees the expression on the reptilian soldier's face and fires, the shot removing the reptile's face. The rest of the team follows suit and fire. Beams of phaser fire fill the corridor, flying in both directions. A minute and a half pass to find all twelve soldier's on the floor, blood splatter covering every wall in view.

"One thing about the Chandraka," Daniel says aloud. "They are so fucking predictable."

"Hoon!" Voltarus yells in distress. The others turn to see Lieutenant Hoon lying on the floor, a four inch diameter hole burned through his chest and his face.

Nire doesn't bother to check his vital signs, she just weeps visibly. The rest of the team stands silently, numb from shock. It takes several minutes before reality snaps back, reality in the form of a shower of blood spraying over Hoon's lifeless body.

Torres' body falls silently, face first on top of Hoon, a look of disbelief glued to his face. His lifeless eyes focused on the hole in his chest. Daniel spins as he falls to the floor, bringing his rifle into firing position as he hits the ground. The rest of the team turns to see two Chandrakan soldiers standing in the corridor several meters beyond the intersection.

The three standing archangel drop to one knee as bolts of plasma zoom over their heads, exploding on the wall behind them. Daniel is the first to fire followed quickly by the others. The two soldiers start to dance involuntarily as phaser beams pierce through their bodies. They are dead before they hit the floor.

Daniel stands, motioning to the others. Voltarus picks up Torres and slings his lifeless body over his shoulder, aiming his rifle in front of him with his free arm. Richards does the same for Hoon. They make their way past the intersection, Daniel on point, followed by Voltarus and Richards with Nire at the rear.

They enter the "mess hall" from the center door with no other obstacles. As Richards and Voltarus quickly make their way across the room to turbolift, Daniel and Nire focus on the two other door-ways behind them.

They enter the turbolift and silently ride it to the surface. The door opens to an empty corridor. They cautiously make their way the several hundred meters to the entry corridor. With no other soldiers in their way they emerge from the dark corridor, it takes several minutes for their eyes to adjust to the light.

Once the adjustment is made they make their way the one point six kilometers to the Deliverance. Ten minutes down the street commotion to the left force the team to stop. Richards and Voltarus put their comrades down gently and take cover, aiming to the left. Nire and Daniel take cover, focusing to the left as well. Several seconds later a drone protrudes from the ally the soldiers are aiming at. It stops several meters past the ally entrance, rotating its turret, scanning the area around it.

Daniel fires when the scanners are aiming toward their ship. The other three fire when he does. They continue firing until the drone explodes in a brilliant flash and thunderous noise.

It takes another ten minutes to get to the ship. They go aboard and prepare for launch. In three minutes the transport is airborne. In seven minutes the tiny ship is entering the hanger bay of the *Tartarus*.

Chapter 10

"Captain's log, stardate 30435.61. The destruction of Chandraka is complete. We mourn the deaths of Lieutenants Maraka Hoon and Pitar Torres, who gave their lives in the fulfillment of the mission. Our next stop... H'Too Bar'klaa."

Atany sits in her chair, staring at Chandar Two on the screen, in quiet contemplation. Fental is doing the same beside her. Both are considering their next moves. Atany straightens up.

"E.T.A. to H'Too Bar'klaa at warp five?" The captain asks.

"Five point eight hours." Levi replies. She thinks for a moment.

"And at warp eight?" She asks.

"Two point two hours." He answers.

"Warp eight, now." She commands. Chandar Two slowly disappears from the screen then the stars become streaks of light.

Hawking leaves the bridge quietly. Fental sees him leave.

"I'm going to the galley for a bite," She tells Atany as she stands.

"Enjoy," Atany replies with a forced yet genuine smile.

"I will," Fental replies with a slight smile, also forced yet genuine. She leaves the bridge.

The door to the turbolift opens two decks below the bridge and Hawking is standing in front of the exit. Fental steps out of the lift, right into Hawking's arms. He kisses her hard and long, his tongue dancing with hers. Their kiss lasts for several minutes.

"What are we going to do about Atany?" Fental asks him.

"I don't know yet," He admits. "We have to keep our eyes open and if we see an advantage, we take it. I don't know when or where or even if we'll find one but we need to pay serious attention."

They walk down the hall, away from any other crewmen. They turn a corner and enter the first room on the left, a laboratory. When the door whooshes closed, Hawking spins Fental to face him, looking deep into her eyes. Without warning he squats down in front of her. He grabs on tightly to the waistband of her uniform slacks on both sides and quickly but carefully slides them down to her ankles along with her panties. He pulls her slacks off over her boots.

He stands, lifting her off her feet and sitting her on the table behind her. She offers no resistance as he lets his trousers drop to his ankles. She now sees that he has gone commando today.

Hawking grabs a handful of Fental's hair and forcefully lays her on the table. She moans in anticipation of what's about to happen. Once her head hits the table she feels the dampness of Hawking's tongue gently caressing her left nipple and a gentle tugging of her right nipple. She feels the heat explode from between her legs as her inner juices drip from her dark hole.

Ari has no problem sinking his large, hard cock into her tight, wet pussy. She moans wildly as his cock sinks all the way in. He thrusts in and out in a rhythm that makes her cum in minutes. He feels her body quiver in orgasmic ecstasy but continues his rhythmic assault.

* * *

Five minutes pass and Hawking feels Fental's body tighten up, ready to explode in orgasm a second time. His thrusts become more forceful as he forces his tongue into her mouth. His complete dominance of her body brings her closer to climax. As the muscles protecting the entrance of her pussy start to tighten around Hawking's hard shaft, preparing to orgasm, Ari begins to feel himself ready to explode. He continues thrusting faster and, as Fental's body explodes in orgasm, so does Hawking's. He continues to kiss her, more gently now, as both their bodies relax from the quick yet intense workout.

"That was awesome," She tells him.

"You were awesome," He replies.

"Let's go get something to eat," She says.

"Absolutely," He responds as he slides his now limp cock out of her.

Nearly two hours later, Fental takes her seat beside the captain. Hawking logs into his station, preparing for the coming battle.

"How long?" Fental asks as she sits.

"Forty-three minutes." Levi answers.

"Go to warp nine point five." Atany orders.

"Now we'll be there in four minutes." The helmsman volunteers.

"When we get there go into a standard orbit," She commands.

The streaking star pattern turns static and a lush, green and blue orb takes up most of the viewscreen. The ship rolls into orbit with no resistance. The captain looks worried.

"This is damned peculiar," She says aloud. "Scan for the appropriate targets and let me know when they're in the firing solution."

"Targets acquired and locked into a firing solution, captain." Sacar says after the ship completes three orbits. There are still no other ships in scanner range.

* * *

"Begin firing," Atany orders and the phaser volleys and torpedo assaults begin. Three full orbits leave most of the targets destroyed and thousands of beings dead with millions more wounded.

"Stop firing," Atany commands with a sense of urgency. "Daniel, Hawking, scan the region. Are there any ships?" Both men begin.

"I'm reading thirteen ships coming from behind the moon. One, seven, two mark zero, one, six." Daniel says with some excitement.

"We can handle them with the Deliverance and the Ex Vee's." Atany replies with confidence.

"Not this, though," Hawking says with panic in his voice. "I've got thirty-nine ships, multiple configurations at two, four, four mark zero, seven, three, coming from behind the planet."

"Fuck this," Atany says calmly. "Levi, get us out of here. Heading zero, two, two mark zero, four, four, warp nine, now!" The ship turns slightly to the right then shoots off at seven hundred and four million kilometers a second.

"Engage the invisibility shields," Atany says aloud.

"Shields engaged." Lieutenant Merah responds. Atany sits back, taking a deep breath and letting out a sigh of relief. Ten minutes pass.

"All stop," Atany orders and Levi complies.

"Are we being pursued?"

"No targets in weapons range," Sacar reports.

"But they are in pursuit," Daniel answers. "Fifty-two ships in pursuit. There are thirty Alliance warships and five science ships, five Utorian warships, three Chandrakan and three Horatha warships as well as two Rillian and four Bar'klaan warships."

"I guess we didn't totally eliminate our opponents." Atany comments with some humor in her voice. It doesn't last long.

"I guess not." Fental replies with a suppressed smile.

"What are they doing?" The captain asks with concern.

"They're getting into formation," Daniel explains. "There are eight ships abreast, six rows high. The science ships are taking positions at the four corners and one is in the center."

"What the fuck are they doing?" She wonders aloud.

"They're setting up a net." Hawking answers and continues. "I'm reading a massive neutrino blanket between the ships. It's a huge net. If we pass through it, even invisible, we'll be detected.

"The net covers half a light year square." Daniel adds.

She sits quietly plotting her next move. Less than five minutes pass.

"Levi, bring us over the net and bring us to the very edge of our weapons range, in line with the science ship in the middle." She orders.

It takes eight minutes for the *Tartarus* to settle into position. On the viewscreen the crew sees the array of ships, a faint blue haze barely visible between them. The *Tartarus* follows, matching speed with the fleet.

"Sacar, lock weapons on the Alliance science ship in the center of the formation, then the Horathan ships."

"I have simultaneous locks on all four ships, captain." Sacar says after several seconds.

"Excellent," She says. "Levi bring us twenty thousand kilometers closer then disengage the invisibility shields. When we're in position, blow those four ships to hell then reengage the invisibility shields and back us off fifty thousand kilometers with a positive zee axis of five thousand kilometers. Got it?" All acknowledge.

"Do it," She says. "Now."

The massive ship becomes visible when it reaches the distance specified by the captain. Bolts of phased plasma, several meters long, and torpedoes light up the space between the armada and the lone Forzak battlecruiser.

At twenty thousand kilometers distance, it takes the first volley about five seconds to reach their targets. In that time three more

● ● ●

volleys are fired and sent along the same flight path as the previous ones.

The Alliance science ship in the center of the array explodes, without warning, in a fierce fireball. Two of the surrounding Alliance warships explode from impact with debris from the science ship. The three Horathan warships explode seconds after the science ship, bringing their total to six ships. The invisibility shields reengage as the ship moves to its new location.

The armada turns to pursue the enemy ship. Arriving at the coordinates their computers say the attack originated, they find nothing but empty space. The fleet holds its position while the captains of each ship confer to decide their next move.

"Lock torpedoes on the remaining science vessels and plot them in a parabolic course." Atany orders.

"Course plotted and laid in." Sacar replies.

"Fire!"

The first torpedoes take out the shields of the science ships, causing power couplings to overload and explode throughout all the ships. The second torpedoes impacts on their hulls, vaporizing the ships instantly.

"Fire full barrage at the Utorian ships," Atany orders next. The ship fires all weapons and, for an instant, becomes visible to the enemy ships thirty thousand kilometers in front of them. Three of the Utorian warships explode under the barrage. The other two blow up as a result of being hit by debris. The remaining Alliance warships maneuver away from the carnage in their midst except one.

"Negative ten thousand kilometers zee axis," The captain commands with a sense of urgency in her voice. The now invisible ship begins to drop. Suddenly the ship rocks violently, sporadic explosions appear across the bridge.

The plan implemented by the other ships captains seems to have worked. When the first ship detected the *Tartarus* they would all fire around the coordinates of the assault's origin. Once impact on the Forzak ship was detected, they would concentrate on that location. It was, in a small way, successful.

"What the hell's happening?" Atany shouts out.

"Apparently they had a contingency plan," Hawking volunteers.

"You think?" She replies with a slight disdain. "Levi, come about one hundred and eighty degrees, warp nine, now."

"Aye, captain," He answers as the ships on the screen shoot off to the left as the *Tartarus* turns hard to the right, hitting warp nine while completing the half circle turn.

"Come to heading two, seven, five mark zero, four, four," Atany orders after twenty seconds. Thirty more seconds pass.

"Bring us around in an arc. Put us twenty thousand kilometers to that fleet's starboard flank." She tells Levi then turns to Daniel. "How badly are we damaged?"

"We have power fluctuations throughout half the ship. The damage we sustained in the last attack has been worsened. There are breaches in the upper assembly above the drive section. Force fields are in place. It's substantial but not detrimental, yet." Daniel tells her.

"What's the repair estimate?" She asks.

"About four hours." He answers.

"Get work crews on it now."

"There on it as we speak."

"All stop until the repairs are complete."

"Captain's log, supplemental. We have completed repairs. Elapse time, four point three hours. Twenty percent of the fleet sent to stop us has been destroyed.

The rest of the fleet is in front of us, unaware of our location."

"Bring us behind the fleet," Atany orders. "Behind the starboard most ships. Twenty thousand kilometers."

"In position," Levi says after several minutes of maneuvering.

"Lock weapons on the four most starboard ships and fire at will. Work to the right." Atany says and the volleys launch from the ship. Firing in the same manner as before, the four volley assault takes out the four targets. Before any of the ships can move, four more are obliterated.

The *Tartarus* rocks once again, more violently than before. A second round hits the battleship before anyone can react, power couplings shorting out in various consoles. From the outside the massive ship flickers into view several times.

"Get us out of here now," Atany commands as the ship rocks again. Levi taps on several controls and the ship streaks away.

"Damage report," She asks.

"Previous hull breaches have been opened again. Force fields are in place but at seventy-seven percent strength." Daniel reports. I'm reading at least three dozen ruptured conduits throughout the ship."

"Get crews on the repairs again." She tells him. "Levi, set a course for H'Too Bar'klaa, warp one point five."

"Aye, captain." He replies. "E.T.A. is three hours, twenty-two minutes." The ship streaks along as the personnel on board repair the damages from the battle. Twenty minutes pass and the repair teams finish changing out the final power couplings. The hull breaches have been sealed and the power levels are stable at eighty-seven percent.

"Entering standard orbit around H'Too Bar'klaa," Levi informs the captain.

"How are our invisibility shields?"

"Fully operational at one hundred percent power," Lieutenant Richards reports. "But I can't estimate how long they'll remain that way."

"Understood," She answers. "Sacar, anything on scanners?"

"System clear, captain," He replies.

"Okay," Atany says calmly. "Commence firing." The weapons fire continuously as the ship orbits the planet. Six orbits devastate all the intended targets.

"Hail what's left of the central government," Atany commands.

"Commissioner Tsokol on the line," Roeton says after a minute.

"What is the meaning of this attack?" The bloodied face on the scream yells in utter defiance.

"Shut the fuck up," Atany tells him. "I am now charge of your planet," She tells him and smiles as shock and disbelief becomes more pronounced on his face.

"You are tasked with cleaning the debris and bodies from our action and informing the remaining populations that I am the sole authority of your world. When we return I will dictate my will to the citizens. Failure to comply will result in the total destruction of your planet. Do you understand?"

"Yes," Tsokol replies. "But why have you done this?"

"Because, my dear commissioner, I can." She motions to Roeton and the screen goes blank for half a second then H'Too Bar'klaa appears. "Captain," Sacar begins. "The armada just came into range. They'll intercept in seventeen minutes."

"What's our status?" She asks.

"Not good enough to take on that many ships directly," Daniel reports.

"Alright then," Atany says. "Get us to Utoria, warp one point five. Let's eliminate the long term threat then we'll take out those ships." Fental looks over at Hawking, wondering how much more killing they must allow. She sees that Hawking's eyes don't hold the answer.

Chapter 11

"Captain's log, stardate 30446.13. We are in orbit around Utoria. Once this planet is under my control, the Brantaxians will be the only threat to us. Complete domination is nearly within my grasp."

"Fire all weapons," Atany says from her command chair. "Firing all weapons," Sacar repeats as he does what's ordered. Wave after wave of phaser bolts and torpedoes race toward the surface. Seconds later massive explosions are visible from the ship. An hour passes as the bombardment continues. Orbit after orbit increase the amount of desolation and death.

It takes another hour for the targets on the surface to be obliterated. The *Tartarus* completes two more orbits, just to be sure. The ship rocks slightly as it starts to leave orbit.

"What was that?" Atany asks after the rocking subsides.

"There are eight ships, twenty thousand kilometers aft." Sacar answers. The ship rocks again. The captain spins so she can see Sacar eye to eye.

"Seven more coming up from under us," He continues to report.

"Fifteen to one," The captain says aloud, to herself. "We don't have time for this right now." She continues. "Helm, get us to the Brantax system, warp six." The stars start to streak.

"E.T.A. is thirty-two minutes." Levi tells her.

The time passes quickly as the different damage control teams check in. The hull breaches have been repaired. The damage is extensive. The breaches, which are sealed for now, can break apart at any moment. The power couplers have all been replaced and the damaged conduits have also been repaired. Since none of the crew has previous experience on any of these systems, no one can predict what will happen when they are put to the test. All the teams finish checking in just as a small dot appears in the center of the viewscreen.

"Approaching Brantax Eleven," Levi says to the captain. "Orbit in twenty seconds." The dot turns into a planet and quickly fills the screen.

"We are being hailed, captain." Lieutenant Roeton Says.

"Audio only," Atany says.

"Unknown vessel," The female voice says with nervousness. "Please activate your transponder and transmit your flight plan."

"Brantax control," Atany says with a pleasant tone. "We are unable to transmit our transponder."

"Unknown vessel, explain." The voice demands.

"Well," Atany says, very pleasantly. "That's a funny story, actually." She pauses for a second. "Since we acquired our vessel, I never thought to look for the transponder transmitter control.

"I cannot allow you clearance to this planet without a transponder," The controller's voice sounding annoyed.

"I'll tell you what we did find though," Atany continues. "We found the controls for the weapons systems." She turns to Sacar. "Fire."

The torpedoes and phaser bolts shoot from the ship and race toward the surface of the planet. Seconds pass while the bridge crew listen to the activity in the control room.

"What's that?" A voice comes over the ship's PA.

"I don't know," Another voice answers. "But it's getting bigger."

"My Gods!" The first voice screams. "It's a phaser bolt!" The dull roar of the phaser bolt hitting the shields is heard.

"Fuck! Torped..." A voice screams but is interrupted by a torpedo impacting on the shields, destroying their generators. The next torpedo directly impacts the room. The screams of the controllers is cut off by the explosions. The channel goes silent as more phaser bolts and torpedoes impact the area.

"Captain, we have a problem!" Sacar says.

"Elaborate." Fental replies.

"Eighteen ships," Sacar explains. "It appears they are trying to surround us in a huge ball."

"We can't fight them like this," Fental says somewhat suggestively.

"Six more ships coming in from Brantax Three." Daniel informs Atany.

"Find a hole and get us out of here," The captain orders, "Get us into the Danarus asteroid field."

"On our way, captain," Levi answers as the stars on the screen start to move left as the ship swings to the right, heading for a gap in the huge ball of warships.

It takes nearly forty minutes before the ship comes out of warp. The asteroid field encompasses the full width of the viewscreen and nearly three quarters of its height, and they are just over two million kilometers from the field's outer edge.

• • •

It takes five minutes before the ship enters the field. It maneuvers carefully around several medium-sized asteroids and a dozen smaller ones, making it five kilometers deep.

Levi finds three asteroids capable of hiding the *Tartarus*, the furthest being three quarters of a lightyear ahead. The captain decides that this is the one. Between them, roughly ten million medium-sized or smaller asteroids, all capable of destroying the ship.

Using the maneuvering thrusters, Levi swings the huge battleship gingerly around each of the drifting rocks and, after almost forty-five minutes, settles in behind the massive rock.

"Long range sensors can scan fifty thousand kilometers beyond the edge of the field." Daniel tells his captain.

"How about us?" She asks. "Are we visible?"

"Negative," He answers. "They come up about thirty thousand kilometers short."

"Very good," She replies. Give me a tactical overview. Three hundred, sixty-five degree view."

"Yes, captain," He answers. It takes about fifteen seconds for the image on the screen to change.

The image is a view of the asteroid field from above with the Tartarus in the center. There are five evenly spaced rings growing out from the silhouette of the ship. The asteroids are shown in outline. The image ends at the end of sensor range.

"While we play cat and mouse with this armada I would like you and Hawking to go over our data." Atany tells Fental. "I need the two of you to determine the amount of damage we inflicted on Brantax Eleven."

"We'll take care of it, captain," Fental answers as she stands. She walks over to the console besides Hawking. She leans in.

"The captain wants us to go over the data we collected at Brantax to determine the extent of our attack. Fental says in a near whisper.

"Okay," He answers as he calls up the data on his screen. They review what little data there is. Thirty minutes pass.

● ● ●

"If we tell her what we found you know she'll insist we go back and finish the job." Hawking says.

"I know, I know," Fental replies. "Give me a minute to think."

"I've got it," Fental says after a few seconds. "I'll take care of Dinema."

The first officer stands and heads back to her seat near the captain.

"What's the good word?" Atany asks.

"Our attack took out the central command structure." Fental begins. "The entire complex was leveled. We also completely destroyed their primary spaceport and we inflicted damage over seventy percent of their auxiliary spaceport. They are no longer a threat."

Excellent," Atany says with a smile. "When we finish off this armada we have one last trip to Utoria then the quadrant is mine."

"Why do we have to go back to Utoria?" Fental asks.

"We were interrupted before we could take out their military training center on their moon. They are the only military force apart from this armada that pose a threat.

"Excellent," Fental acknowledges. "With everything going on I completely forgot about that."

"No worries, my friend," She answers and focuses her attention on the screen.

It takes nearly thirteen minutes before the first signal appears on the screen. After that, a new signal appears every few seconds. The dots come on and go off of the screen so often that the ship's computers could not get an accurate count.

Twenty minutes after the first signal appeared on the screen, a fleet of five ships, flying in loose formation, enter the field, heading toward the rogue ship.

"Who are they?" Atany asks.

"One Alliance science ship and four Alliance warships," Daniel reports. "Three are *Barrage* class ships and one is *Defiance* class."

"How do we take them out without giving away our position?" Atany says aloud but to herself. Seconds tick by in silence.

"Captain," Hawking breaks the silence. "I have an idea."

"What is it, commander?"

"Look at the two asteroids in front of our hiding spot." He begins. "We can creep out starboard and stay behind the one on the right. Focus our tractor beam to push the one on the left into the five ships. They won't see us because of the asteroid and from outside of the field it will look like an accidental collision."

"Great idea," Atany says. "Helm, tactical, do it."

The huge ship glides to the right and comes out from behind the massive rock. The blue, shimmering tractor beam shoots from the nose of the ship and impacts the five million ton rock indicated by Hawking.

The huge rock moves to the left, slowly at first. It picks up speed as the tractor beam continues pushing. After twenty seconds the beam shuts down and the Forzak battlecruiser slips back behind the asteroid.

The tactical display on the screen shows the five ships approaching in a much tighter formation. The image of the moving rock is closing in on them from behind a slightly bigger asteroid.

The rock comes out from behind the larger asteroid and slams into the ship on the right. The ship explodes as the rock fractures. The larger of the pieces continues into the next ship in line.

The bridge crew watch as the third dot maneuvers hard to the left, right into the fourth vessel. The fifth ship turns hard starboard to escape but the explosion caused by the collision of the two ships sends it spiraling out of control, right into another asteroid. In less than thirty seconds all five ships are gone.

"Holy shit," Atany says in disbelief. "It worked."

"Never a doubt," Hawking says, an expression of relief sweeps across his face.

"Nice," Fental says quietly.

"Now we have to deal with the rest of those ships." Atany continues. "How many are out there, Daniel?"

"Scanners show Three Alliance warships, three Alliance science ships, three Chandrakan battleships and four Bar'klaan ships." He replies.

"Ten warships and three science vessels," Atany clarifies as she sits back in her chair.

The dots, representing the enemy ships, dance around the outer edge of the field. The *Tartarus* sits quietly in the center of the screen.

"Can we leave this field from any other direction?" The captain asks.

"No," Daniel answers. "The asteroids are too cluttered together for this ship to get through."

"Daniel," Hawking interrupts. "Can you plot a course out of here that is the least cluttered and overlay it on the viewscreen?"

"Give me a minute," Daniel replies. It takes three minutes and the graphics on the screen rotate to show the asteroid field from a side view.

A blue line protrudes from the *Tartarus*, going up. It zigzags three times before exiting the field.

"There you go, Commander," Daniel says.

"Thank you," Hawking says as he buries his face into his scanner.

"Captain," He says after about a minute and a half.

"What's your idea?" She asks in response.

"If we engage the invisibility shields then use the tractor beam to move the three asteroids blocking Daniel's escape route, we can maneuver out of the field. We can then swing around and destroy the fleet."

"The fleet will notice asteroids moving around, don't you think?" Levi inquires.

"Not if we move them slow enough. They'll appear to be in a gravity well." Hawking explains.

"We'll go with that plan, Dinema orders. "Unless someone has a better idea." The captain looks around the room. There are no other ideas.

"Initiate the invisibility shields," Atany commands. "Levi, bring us up to the first asteroid then initiate the tractor beam and move the first one. You take care of that, Ari."

The now cloaked battlecruiser slowly tilts its nose in an upward direction. It moves forward as the thrusters fire. As the ship approaches the massive rock, the tractor beam shoots from its emitter array.

For the first few seconds there is no reaction but, as the beam continues, the asteroid starts to move. Ten seconds later the beam shuts off.

The ship continues to glide past the slow moving rock and a cluster of asteroids on the right.

The Tartarus flies along unmolested for two minutes when the tractor beam hits the asteroid in front of the ship. Like before, the rock moves slowly out of the way and the ship coasts by.

"Is there any indication that the fleet knows we're on the move?" Atany asks, turning to face her husband.

"Not at all," Daniel answers. "They're still swarming around the area we went in from."

The ship passes the second point and, still under thruster control, cruises for nearly two minutes. The third asteroid comes into range on Hawking's scanner and he engages the tractor beam. Several seconds pass and the asteroid starts to move.

The ship passes the asteroid with a few meters to spare. The ship continues to travel through the asteroid field for another eight minutes.

It exits the field and starts a long, slow arc to come up on the port flank of the enemy fleet. Estimated time to assault, six minutes.

The main viewscreen is returned to the image of the space in front of the Forzak ship. As the seconds tick by, the asteroid field appears back on the screen, taking up one third of the screen, from the left side.

It takes nearly five minutes before the tiny warships come into view. The bridge crew tense up for the coming battle. Another minute passes.

"Sacar," Atany says. "Lock on to the science vessels first. Take them out as soon as you can."

A volley of weapons fire races through space toward the unsuspecting ships. As the two science ships explode in balls of fire, the rest of the fleet turn toward the *Tartarus*. Three more volleys are fired from the nacelles and the ship turns starboard sharply.

As the ship turns to port, two of the Alliance warships explode in brilliant light. Phaser fire from the remaining ships of the fleet rock the Forzak ship. Another three volley burst takes out two of the Chandrakan battleships. The third Chandrakan ship is hit by the twin shockwaves of the explosions and loses its shields. Sporadic explosions are visible through hull breaches. It starts to limp away from the battle.

A five volley burst is now launched against the remaining fleet. Seconds later the four Bar'klaan warships explode without warning. The Chandrakan ship damaged earlier is also destroyed. The last remaining Alliance science ship and warship go to warp before the *Tartarus* can destroy them.

"Where did they go?" Atany asks.

"Unknown," Daniel answers. "They went to warp before I could track their trajectory."

"No worries," She responds. "I'm sure we haven't seen the last of them.

Set a course back to Utoria, warp two. Have Benjamin organize damage control parties to check the impact areas."

• • •

The Forzak battlecruiser turns slightly to port as it noses downward. It blasts into a flash as the warp engines engage, sending the massive ship hurtling through space.

Chapter 12

"Captain's log, stardate 30454.28. We will be in orbit around the moon of Utoria in twenty minutes. This will be the biggest challenge to date. The soldiers of Utoria are trained and stationed on the moon complex. We have no idea how many soldiers will be waiting for our arrival. I pray to the Gods for a favorable outcome."

"Sensor readings?" Atany asks.

"Can't tell anything," Daniel tells her. "Not even these sensors can penetrate the complex. I don't know how many, if any, lifeforms are in waiting."

"Is there an external force field?" She inquires.

"No," He replies. "At least not that these sensors can detect."

"Levi, one half impulse," The captain orders. "Daniel, get your archangels together and devise an assault plan. Have the Ex Vee pilots check their crafts for battle. Put us in a geosynchronous orbit opposite the moon base."

• • •

Rigel and Jasmine head down to their fighters and start their preflight checklists. It takes nearly an hour for the two women to go over all thing items.

"Rigel to bridge," The female fighter pilot says into the communications panel in the wall by the entry hatch.

"Bridge here," Atany's voice sounds back.

"Ex Vees are ready to go." She says.

"Excellent," The captain replies. "The archangels are still planning their assault. Would you and Jasmine run down the *Deliverance* preflight checklist and make sure it's up to par?"

"Will do, captain," Rigel says. "Give us about an hour and a half and we'll be all set."

"Thanks," The captain replies. "When you're finished join Daniel and the archangels in the conference room for support instruction. Out."

Daniel is at the head of the conference table surrounded by the remaining archangels. Lieutenant Commander Nire and Lieutenant Richards are seated on his left and Lieutenant Commander Fental and Lieutenant Voltarus are on his right.

"The base is ten levels deep," Daniel tells his crew. "Each level is circular with a diameter of five kilometers."

"That's one big base," Voltarus exclaims.

"Yes it is," Daniel replies. "And we don't know how many people are waiting for us."

The five spend the next three hours devising a plan of attack. They cover, what they believe, is every contingency they can think of. Rigel and Jasmine enter the room.

"Welcome, ladies," Daniel says with a smile.

"Thank you," Both answer.

"All three ships are ready to go." Rigel tells him.

"Excellent," He replies then continues, "Have a seat. We need your input on your support and separate assault."

The seven spend the next hour and a half working out the assault details. Everything is covered from launch until landing. When they are finished they leave the conference room and head to the hangerbay.

The attack force turns the final corner and, as they approach to doors, the *Tartarus* rocks so violently that half the crewmembers fall to the floor. Fental staggers to her feet and, as she activates the intercom panel on the wall by the doors, the ship rocks again.

"Fental to bridge," She says into the unit. "What's happening?"

"Another attack fleet," Atany's voice sounds as the ship rocks again, the lights flickering this time.

"Everyone report to your duty stations on the double," Fental says and the seven scatter to their assigned stations.

The turbolift door opens to the bridge, which is bathed in smoke from electrical fires caused by system overloads. Fental, Daniel, Rigel, Jasmine and Richards take their posts. The ship rocks again.

"Levi," Atany shouts. "Evasive maneuvers."

"Sacar, Korah, fire at will." Fental shouts out.

"Daniel, status," Atany shouts as the ship rocks again.

The massive battlecruiser nimbly zigzags across the heavens, not only side to side but up and down as well. Phaser fire and torpedoes fly in every direction, daring any of the other ships to approach.

"There are seven ships," Daniel reports. "Five *Barrage* class Alliance ships and two Rillian warships."

"Helm, come around to three, three, six mark zero, eight, two." Atany commands after studying a console on her armrest.

"Tactical, fire as they come to bear," Atany orders next. "All weapons starboard."

The Forzak warship turns tightly to the left and angles nose down, nearly straight down. It speeds straight toward to enemy fleet, splitting it into two groups. The weapons on the right fire four volleys in repetition, destroying two of the Alliance ships and both of the Rillian ships.

The ship turns hard right and angles nose up at forty-five degrees. The ship rocks forcefully as consoles short out all around the bridge.

"Get damage control teams to work," Atany says to Roeton, who acknowledges her command.

"Bring us around one, eight, zero mark zero." She orders. The big ship does a half circle and approaches the last three ships directly in front of them.

"Sacar, take out the lead ship," She says. The Alliance warship explodes under the assault.

"Open hailing frequencies," She continues.

"Open, captain," Roeton replies.

"This is Captain Dinema Atany calling the two remaining Alliance warships." There is no answer for one and a half minutes.

"This is Captain Atany, you have thirty seconds to respond."

"This is Captain Gareth of the space cruiser, *Soothsayer*," The disembodied voice speaks out over the communications system. "You are hereby ordered to stand down and prepare to be boarded."

"Captain, captain," Atany says laughing at the request. "You misunderstand why I'm contacting you."

"Enlighten me, captain," The voice says.

"I am offering amnesty to any member of your crew wiling to pledge allegiance to me."

"Fuck you, captain," The voice says.

"Not today," Atany replies calmly, quietly as she motions to Sacar. The ship on the right explodes from a double volley of firepower.

"The captain of the other ship is hailing," Roeton says.

"Open channel," She orders and he complies. "This is Captain Atany. Captain Gareth has sealed your fate. My apologies. Out."

She motions to Sacar, who activates the weapons systems. The ship explodes.

"Now," Atany says. "Get us to that moon. Archangels go." The crew complies.

Ten minutes pass when the outer hangerbay doors open. The two Ex Vees and the *Deliverance* drop out. The three ships clear the Tartarus and run up to full speed. In seven minutes the ships are fifty meters from the surface of the moon, the top level of the moon base comes into view on the edge of the horizon.

"Here we go," Rigel says over her intercom.

"I see it," Jasmine confirms.

"So do I," Fental, now piloting the *Deliverance*, acknowledges.

The minutes pass as the three ships get closer. The Deliverance slows slightly, allowing the fighters to speed ahead and draw fire. The targeting scanners show the edge of the base is five seconds out. All systems are green, which indicates no weapons or scanners are trying to lock on, which confuses and scares Rigel.

The two Ex Vees do a flyby. Everything is still. There are no shields, no torpedoes and no phaser fire. They see the command center in the middle of the huge circle. They also notice an antennae array at four points around the base.

"This is not good," Rigel says.

"What do you think it means?" Jasmine asks.

"I don't know," Rigel answers. "But I have a bad feeling about this."

After passing over the base the two ships veer off in opposite directions. The *Deliverance* flies over the base then starts a long, wide loop. The three ships converge one hundred kilometers away from the base, déjà vu filling their senses.

On the second pass Rigel takes out the array on the left while Jasmine takes out the one on the right. The *Deliverance* takes out the command center. The three ships perform the same maneuvers and line up for another pass.

This time Rigel takes the lead with the *Deliverance* in the middle and Jasmine taking up the rear. Rigel takes out the two remaining arrays. Fental sets the *Deliverance* down on one of the three landing pads. Jasmine flies over, ready to shoot down anything trying to interfere with the mission.

Lieutenant Richards hacks into the Utorian computer controls and remotely accesses the landing pad airlock controls. The landing pad slowly drops below the surface of the moon. As soon as the ship gets underground a set of doors close above it.

"Okay, ladies," Daniel says to Rigel and Jasmine. "Land on the pads and Richards will activate the airlock system."

"Will do," Rigel replies.

"Let you know when I'm there," Jasmine responds.

The two fighters, flying side by side, break away and set down on their respective pads within seconds of each other.

"I'm down," Rigel says.

"So am I," Jasmine says right after. Within five seconds, the two pads slowly recede into the huge rock. When the outer doors lock above them the bay pressurizes. When the outside atmosphere is able to sustain life the hangerbay door, leading to the corridor, opens.

Rigel and Jasmine, both alone, cautiously enter the corridor, heading in the direction they believe they'll find the *Deliverance* crew. It takes about twenty-five minutes before all members of the assault team are together.

The five archangels start to clear each room in a systematic method, Rigel and Jasmine covering their backs. They pass a turbolift twenty meters down the hall. They access the lift and, when it arrives, they lock it in the open position, stranding it on the second level.

The rooms they clear are all offices and storage for supplies for those offices. As they pass turbo lifts they access them. When the lifts arrive they are locked out like the first one. When they completed the full level, which took nearly seven hours, they stop at the turbolift closest to the landing pad where the *Deliverance* is berthed.

"Rigel, Jasmine," Daniel starts. "You two stay here. If there are any soldiers on the lower levels they'll be forced up on this turbolift, right to you."

"Why wouldn't they just go to level one?" Jasmine asks.

"When the *Deliverance* took out the command center, we opened the main corridor to the vacuum of space. The computer's safety protocols won't allow the lift door to open to a vacuum." Richards explains.

"They'll come out on this level," Daniel says. "Right into the two of you ladies."

"We've got this," Rigel says as she looks at Jasmine. "Don't we?"

"We do," Jasmine answers somewhat unsure. "Yes, we do." More confident now. The two women take up positions across the hall, opposite the lift door. Daniel looks with approval as the five enter the lift. The door closes.

The door opens on level ten. The room is gigantic, one third the size of the full level with the ceiling about fifteen meters high. The decor is that of an open field, complete with rolling hills and trees. The room is dark, lit only by the stars and twin moons projected on the ceiling.

The team exits the lift in a modified flanking formation, making their way cautiously across the field. Midway across the field, spotlights illuminate the five archangels. They drop to the ground as phaser bolts fly just over their heads.

The archangels concentrate their phaser fire into the tree line. Daniel and Nire fire at the lights shining on them while Fental, Voltarus and Richards fire between the lights. After nearly ten minutes of battle the last of the lights explodes into darkness.

The archangels cease fire, allowing the remaining enemy soldiers to give away their positions. As they fire, the archangels track the flashes from the rifle barrels. Fental takes two shots, dropping two Utorians. In the moonlight the two silhouetted soldiers can be seen flying backward from her shots.

Fire from the tree line lasts for another two minutes. Daniel looks at Fental, who nods then looks back down through her sights. This time she fires three shots, spaced two seconds apart. Phaser fire comes from the tree line again, sporadic now.

Fental takes two more shots. An eerie silence sweeps across the room. They remain still for several minutes. Seeing no movement and hearing no sounds, the five cautiously stand. Staying crouched, they move toward the tree line.

Reaching the inside line of trees, the team stumbles across Fental's targets, all seven of them. Daniel smiles, proud of his student.

"Hell of a shot," Nire says to Dutona.

"Yeah, no shit." Voltarus adds.

"Thanks," Fental says. "I had a great teacher." She looks at Daniel with a smile. They stumble across the soldiers taken out in the initial firefight. There are nine others, strewn around the searchlights.

They make their way to the wall and find a door half a kilometer from where they started. The door opens, revealing a short corridor. There is a door at the other end. The five enter the room. The door closes behind them, bathing the corridor in a dull, low light. They walk the few steps to the opposite side of the corridor.

The door opens and the five are blinded by the brightness enveloping them. It takes a few minutes before they can see what they're stepping into. They take a second to mentally prepare then enter.

This room is a suburban neighborhood, complete with streets, houses and a bright, blue sky.

"If I didn't know better, I'd never believe we were underground." Nire says with admiration.

* * *

"No shit," Voltarus replies. "I keep expecting to see kids and pets come out."

"No doubt," Richards adds, awe in his voice.

"It'll take us days to search all these houses," Daniel says. "We've got to go down every street and try to draw any soldiers in this arena."

Voltarus takes out a tricorder and slowly spins in a circle. The screen on his tricorder displays an aerial view of the area they're in.

"We've got twenty-four kilometers of roads to cover," Voltarus says.

"Then let's get started," Daniel tells them.

The team covers street after street, kilometer by kilometer. It takes nearly four hours for the team, broken into two groups, to cover the area. The silence makes everyone uneasy. They reunite and find the door on the opposite wall. They enter the short corridor, the door closing behind them.

The door opens to a locker room. Along the wall, on both sides of the door, are about a dozen spacesuits. In the center of the room, on each side of the door, are long benches. On the wall five meters in front of them is another door, this one has a window in it, opening into an airlock. To the left and right of the door and running the ten meters to the end of the walls, are windows.

Beyond the window the entire section is a simulation of outer space.

"Well, looks like this level is clear," Fental says.

"How can you be so sure?" Richards asks.

"Look around," Fental answers. "There are no missing spacesuits."

"Good eye," Daniel tells her. Let's make our way to the turbolift."

The lift door opens one level up, into a tropical rain forest. The team exits as before, anticipating another attack. Everything is uncomfortably quiet. They follow the contour of the outer wall until they reach the wall separating the rooms.

The five follow this wall until they reach the door to the next room. Scans reveal that the forest takes up half of the level but nothing on the other side. As before, the team enters the corridor and cross to the opposite door. The door opens to a room similar to the one below. Rows of spacesuits line the walls on both sides of the door. Two benches are in the same locations as the others. The airlock door is in the same location.

The only noticeable difference is what lies beyond the two large windows. Rather than the dark vacuum of space, the view is water. Millions of gallons of water fill the room, artificial light illuminating the clear liquid. Again, all the suits are in place. The team returns to the jungle, heading for the turbolift.

Voltarus is walking point, the rest of the team following several meters behind. Nire takes up the rear. They make their way silently through the woods. Daniel, who is in line behind Voltarus, is suddenly knocked to the ground, his face and uniform covered in blood and brain matter.

Voltarus falls to the ground, his head nothing but a bloody stump. The sound of the phaser rifle is heard as he falls. Fental fires at the flash and a scream is heard just before a dull thud. A half dozen flashes appear in a staggered line about fifteen meters to the right. The archangels drop and return fire, Fental being the only one not to fire blindly.

As the enemy soldiers fire, Fental focuses on the muzzle flash of the rifles and fires one shot. She stays focused for several seconds, making sure the target is neutralized then moves on to the next flash.

In five minutes the eerie quietness, experienced earlier, returns as the firing stops. They make their way past the corpses of the enemy and enter the turbolift, their heads hanging low, depression and anger over their loss setting in.

"I know this sucks," Daniel says. "But we need to stay focused on the mission or we could all end up like Voltarus."

"We'll be ready," Richards says. "When that door opens we'll be ready."

The team steps out of the turbolift and begins clearing the floor. This level is nothing but laboratories. Of the thirty labs on the level, ten of them are equipped with sets of adjustable chairs, all with ankle and wrist restraints.

"What do you think they did in here?" Richards asks Nire, the medic.

"I don't know," Nire answers. "But by the looks of this equipment it couldn't have been good."

"Where are all the soldiers?" Fental asks. "There have to be more than just the handful we ran into."

"I'm sure there are," Daniel states. "On the levels above us, no doubt. Keep a sharp eye out. Let's move."

The door opens to another level of laboratories. The four clear the rooms one by one. They slowly make their way around the complex with no resistance. They find themselves once again entering the turbolift.

Level six opens to a parade ground with rows of bleachers against the left wall and half way down the front and back walls. Along the back wall is a hatch the size of six regular doors. This hatch starts near the corner of the right wall, directly across from the turbolift.

"Through there," Daniel says, motioning to the hatch. The four start walking across the open floor watching all four sides as the cross. After several minutes they make it to the hatch. Richards manipulates the controls and the door opens with a nearly silent scratching sound.

They enter the next room, a sort of staging area for ceremonies conducted in the parade ground room. Still no signs of life. They enter the adjoining room, a large room with rows of tables. At the far end there is a long, rectangular opening in the wall, exposing another room beyond.

"This must be the mess hall," Fental says.

"I believe you're right," Daniel replies.

"Then that must be the kitchen," Fental points to the room beyond the opening in the wall. The four walk to the door besides the rectangular opening and enter.

The room is full of stoves, grills, ovens and other equipment used for preparing meals. They carefully make their way across the room and through the door at the opposite end. This door opens to a long, narrow corridor.

They continue down the corridor for several kilometers. The corridor ends at a door on the left wall. It opens to the parade ground room, right on the side of the turbolift. They enter the lift.

The four exit onto level five. The entire level is row after row of storerooms. There are several large freezers, as well as a dozen smaller ones, containing various meats. The bulk of the storerooms contain dry goods. They search the entire level, room by room, until they return to the active turbolift.

Going up a level, they exit onto another floor full of storerooms. In the first of these rooms the archangels find Utorian uniforms.

"This must be the quartermaster supply rooms," Richards says.

"If this is quartermaster supply rooms we've got to keep an eye out for weapons and ammo." Daniel tells them. Each archangel picks a corridor and head down, checking the rooms on each side as they make their way.

Daniel," Fental shouts from near the end of her row. "You need to see this." In less than a minute he arrives, as does Nire and Richards. The large room is full of phaser rifles and power supply packs.

"Nice find," Daniel says.

R. N. CHEVALIER

"Yeah," Fental agrees. "But come across the hall." She leads the way into another room, this one only half full.

"Now this is disconcerting," Daniel says.

"Yeah it is," Fental replies. "If we assume that the missing weapons are with soldiers here with us, I'm guessing there are still about twenty soldiers still lying in wait for us."

"Grab a fresh weapon," Daniel says as he takes a phaser rifle from the rack in front of him. He slings it over his shoulder and picks up a second. The rest follow suit as he loads the one in his hands with a fully charged power pack. He takes three more power packs and heads for the door, looking out carefully before exiting.

The three archangels follow him out and they finish clearing the level. They make their way back to the turbolift and head to the next level. The lift door opens and the four step out.

They are in a corridor similar to the one above, where Rigel and Jasmine are waiting. They break into two groups and head in opposite directions. Checking every room, the teams find crew quarters, with several common shower rooms and bathrooms.

The two teams rendezvous on the far end of the complex. They stand where the concentric corridor meets with the corridor that goes straight to the turbolift, right through the center of the level.

"Did you two encounter any Utorians?" Daniel asks.

"No," Fental answers. "Not yet."

"This corridor is the last one on this level," Richards says after checking his tricorder.

"The last twenty are either here or upstairs," Daniel says. "So be careful going back to the turbolift." They start walking cautiously down the dark corridor.

Everything is still and silent as the archangels walk down the hall, two on each side of corridor, near the walls. The turbolift door comes into view. The team slows down to a near crawl.

The silence is shattered by the brilliant explosion of weapons fire connecting with the bulkhead inches from Daniel's face.

• • •

"Aarrgghh!!" Daniel lets out a scream of pain as the hot phaser plasma and hotter metal fragments pepper his face, blinding his right eye.

Daniel falls to the floor, cupping his eye with both hands, silently coping with the pain in his face. Nire, who is several meters behind Fental, against the opposite wall, drops to her hands and knees and crawls to Daniel's aid.

Fental, who is on the opposite side of the corridor, drops to her left knee as Richards, who is several meters behind Daniel, drops to his right knee.

Another brilliant flash explodes inches from Daniel's head. Nire throws her hands over her head, protecting her face. He doesn't notice.

"They're in the ceiling ductwork," Fental says aloud.

"Got 'em," Richards says. They both fire into the ceiling, not at the vent opening but in the ceiling between the vent and turbolift. Muffled cries of pain can be heard.

The phased energy bolts pierce the ceiling ductwork leaving ten centimeter holes. After twenty seconds of continuous fire from two rifles leaves the ceiling littered with holes form the duct vent to the turbolift, blood dripping from dozens of these holes.

"How is he?" Fental asks in a slight panic.

"Flash burns and there are fragments in his eye." Nire tells her. There is quiet.

"Can you treat him now?"

"Yeah," She answers. "As long as the shooting's over."

"Seems to be," She replies. "Richards, you're with me. We're going to check the duct." She turns to Nire. "Treat him now. We're not finished."

Fental and Richards quickly make their way the five meters down the hall while Nire treats Daniel's injury. The only motion ahead of them is the blood dripping from the holes in the ceiling.

Once under the vent panel, Richards bends his leg at the knee and his upper body forward. He nods to Fental. She steps on his bent knee, using it as a step. She then places her knee on his shoulder, lifting herself on his shoulders.

She cautiously lifts the vent panel, sending the barrel of her rifle in ahead. Raising her head into the duct she sees three Utorians laying in the ductwork. They are dead. She jumps off of Richard's shoulder.

"Three," She says to the others. "They're dead." She looks at Daniel. "How are you feeling?"

"I'll be good," He answers. "But with one eye, I need for you to take command of the squad."

"No problem," She replies. "One more level, a dozen and a half more enemy soldiers, I love this shit." She smiles wide. Daniel stands, smiling back, and the four make their way to the turbolift.

When the door opens, the view isn't what they expected. Six Utorians lay dead on the floor. Across the corridor, still in the position she was in when they left, Rigel is slumped in her corner, four phaser blasts cross her chest. Jasmine is nowhere in sight.

"Circle 'round," Fental says as she leaves the lift and as each exit they face outward, looking for the enemy. Fental makes her way to Rigel, checking for signs of life. There are none. Daniel, Nire and Richards check the Utorians. They are all dead.

"This way," Fental orders, motioning to the left. The four slowly make their way down the outer corridor. They check room after room, all of them crew quarters. Half a kilometer down the hall they stumble upon four more bodies, all Utorian, all dead.

"Where the hell is Jasmine?" Nire asks.

"I don't know," Fental says. "I hope she's okay."

"So do I," Richards interjects. "We should find her and get out of here."

"Good idea," Fental replies. "We should call you captain obvious."

"Yeah," He responds. "Very funny." The four continue down the hall.

The team makes it half way around the complex without any sign of Jasmine, or the other six or so Utorian soldiers. Rather than come down the central corridor, the four continue along the outer concentric corridor.

The door opens as the team prepares to enter. Phaser blasts fly from the open entryway, exploding against the opposite wall. A woman's scream is heard during the barrage.

"Jasmine!" Fental shouts during a lull in the shooting.

"Fental?" Jasmine sounds surprised. "Is that you?"

"Yes," Fental replies. "Stop shooting."

"Sorry," Jasmine states. "Come in, hurry." The four enter the room, the door closing behind them.

"What happened?" Daniel asks.

"About two hours ago the turbolift door opened," Jasmine begins, still shaken. "We thought it was you guys. As soon as Rigel saw they were Utorians she took out two. She was hit with fire before I could take out the rest. I started running. I took out the soldiers in the hall then ran again. I ducked in here to catch my breath."

"Do you know how many are left?" Fental asks her.

"Three," Jasmine answers. "Only three."

"Daniel," Fental starts with a worried tone. "There's a huge problem."

"What's the problem?"

"This complex is designed to house, what, forty thousand troops? We've encountered thirty? Where are the rest?"

"Good question," A look of concern sweeps across his face. "Let's find these last three and get back to the *Tartarus*. We'll figure it out up there."

"Helm, bring us around. One, seven, one mark eighty-eight!" Atany screams above the sound of plasma escaping from conduits and the crackle of electricity from shorting panels.

"Yes, captain," Levi shouts back and the big ship starts to arc around.

● ● ●

"Sacar, lock phasers on the two closest ships and fire," The captain yells.

"Firing phasers," Sacar says as the ship starts to list to the right. There is an explosion on the bridge.

"Two enemy ships destroyed," Sacar reports. "There are four left."

"Korah, lock torpedoes on targets," Atany orders.

"The explosion we experienced killed Korah," Sacar informs Atany. "I need a few seconds to reconfigure my console."

"Levi," Atany shouts. "Get him those few seconds!"

"Aye, aye, captain," Levi replies. For several seconds the ship remains still.

"Console set," Sacar says. "Firing." One of the two ships on the screen explodes.

"Three more ships coming from behind the moon," Hawking shouts out.

"Fuck!" Atany screams with aggravation in her voice. "We'll deal with them soon enough. Lock on to the closest sips and blow them to hell."

Sacar fires phasers and another Utorian warship disintegrates in a brilliant fireball.

"Five left," Sacar says as the *Tartarus* rocks heavily.

"Correction," Hawking interjects. "There are four left." Confusion shows on Atany's face.

"Now there are three left," Hawking continues.

"We're being hailed," Roeton says.

"Open channel," Atany replies.

"This is the *Deliverance*," Daniels voice booms on the bridge. "Now that we've taken care of the last two Utorian ships, you think we can come aboard?"

"Permission granted," Atany says with a huge smile. "Get damage control parties out to inspect and repair."

"Benjamin reports three of his staff are in sickbay. Several people will be up here soon." Roeton responds.

• • •

Five minutes pass in stillness and quiet. Three crewmen from engineering come off of the turbolift and head straight for the most seriously damaged part of the bridge, Korah's station.

"Sacar, You and Levi get Korah's body to sickbay." They acknowledge and comply, leaving the bridge via the rear corridor. Several minutes pass and the turbolift door opens again.

Atany runs up to Daniel, throwing her arms around him tightly. She gives him a long hard kiss. Hawking, seeing Fental, stands and kisses her deeply. Richards and Jasmine take their duty stations. After nearly a minute the four take their stations.

"What happened to your eye?" Atany asks as she touches the bandage wrapped around Daniel's head.

"Flash burn and a few metal fragments hit me," He explains. "It looks worse than it is. I'll be fine."

"Are you sure?"

"It's all good, baby," He reassures her. Relief sweeps across her face.

"Report," Atany orders, now focused on the tasks at hand.

"There are no enemy ships in sensor range," Hawking reports.

"Great," She answers. Now, what happened on the moon base?"

"There were less than fifty soldiers. We took them out but we lost Rigel and Voltarus."

"We lost Korah during the last battle," She informs her shipmates. "What's wrong, Fental?" She asks her first officer, seeing the anger on her face.

"I have to ask you, captain," Fental begins. "We've followed you since we found this ship. We've had several issues and now we've lost five crewmates in the last few days along with the hundreds of thousands on the ships and planets we've destroyed, I've got to know... Is it worth it?"

"Yes, it is," Atany answers with a smile. Disgust now sweeping across Fental's face.

"How do you justify all this death?" The first officer continues.

"I can justify this by reminding you of the billions of lives that will be spared once I am in control." Atany says boastfully. The only things stopping total peace in the quadrant are about fifty more warships. Once they're gone there will be no more wars, no more death due to violence."

"Until you decide someone needs to die?"

"Of course," The captain replies coldly, with a smile. Others in the room share Fental's feelings but no one dare face off against the captain now. The two women stand, eyes locked together.

"Roeton," Atany says without breaking her glare. "Get me a damage report from Benjamin." It takes about thirty seconds.

"Benjamin reports repairs will take about fifteen hours. He recommends we do not go to warp until the repairs are complete."

"Lieutenant Richards, set a course back to our planetoid at one half impulse. Avoid any and all ships for now."

"Aye, captain," He replies. He keys in the appropriate commands and the ship speeds away.

● ● ●

Chapter 13

"Captain's log, stardate 30492.12. The Utorian training facility located on their moon has been destroyed. About fifty warships stand in my way of total domination of the quadrant. Repairs are nearly complete. I plan on taking the ships out a few at a time. It begins in a few hours."

"What have you got left to repair?" Atany asks into her armrest.

"We've got a couple of power shunts on deck twelve," Benjamin starts. "As well as a hull breach and two invisibility shield emitters above the drive section. We'll have to stop when we repair the emitters."

"Understood," She replies. "Contact me when we need to stop."

"Yes, captain," Atany deactivates the intercom. It takes two hours.

"Captain," Roeton says. "Benjamin says his teams are ready to repair the emitters. We need to stop."

"Levi, all stop." Atany orders.

"All stop," He replies and manipulates the controls. The great ship slowly comes to a stop.

"All stopped, captain." Levi announces after a minute.

"Inform engineering," Atany tells Roeton and he complies.

The two teams of two beam to the outside of the ship, one team aft and one midship. They continue working for nearly three quarters of an hour.

"Lieutenant Aurora to Commander Benjamin, we're ready to be beamed back inside." The engineer's mate says, floating just under the ship with Bildar Tac, another engineer's mate. They sparkle out of existence, materializing on the transporter platform.

"This is Xandaric," A strangely mechanical voice sounds through the ship several minutes later. "Vorgar and I are ready to beam back." They dematerialize from the underside of the ship.

The two members of the damage control team begin rematerializing as the ship rocks violently for several seconds. The blue haze of the annular confinement beam starts to flicker as three transporter pads, including the two in use, shower sparks from under the platform.

The annular confinement beam fades away completely and the two blue, sparkling silhouettes start to disperse, separating and floating around the transporter room.

"Oh, fuck no!" Lieutenant Commander Reuben, manning the transporter room for this mission, screams in wild panic. He manipulates the controls and slides the controllers, activating the unit again. The pads in the floor of the platform begin shooting sparks once again, the sound of electricity loudly crackling in the air.

The ship rocks again, more violently than the last time, causing the transporter unit to power down for several seconds.

"Fuck!" The night duty communications officer screams as he tries to lock onto the two crewmen caught in mid transport.

"Reuben to bridge," He says, panic thick in his voice.

"What's wrong, Reuben?" Atany's strained voice comes through the console's speaker. "We're kinda busy up here." The ship rocks again.

"I was in the middle of transporting the damage control team aboard when we were hit the first time." He says into the console. "I've lost them, captain."

"Understood," She replies somewhat solemn, bowing her head for a moment. She looks up and at Fental, feeling her icy stare. She is right. Her eyes lock onto Fental's, whose cold stare is contrary to the sadness of losing two crewmates. It lasts about two seconds. The ship rocks hard.

"Bring us to course zero, seven, five mark six, two." Atany orders. "Fire as targets come to bear."

"Aye," Sacar says as he locks the weapons on target. "Firing."

On the screen, one ship explodes and two others are damaged but functional. The *Tartarus* turns, bringing the two damaged ships into view. Weapons fire tear through the hulls of both ships, vaporizing them in a ball of fiery brilliance.

The *Tartarus* turns again, bringing four ships into view on the viewscreen. Sacar fires and one ship explodes as a second is damaged. The other two take evasive action and fire on the Forzak starship. The ship rocks to the right.

Sacar fires again and one of the two ships disintegrates. The ship rocks slightly to the left and, when it levels out, Sacar fires two more volleys. The damaged ship vaporizes as torpedoes rip through the hull of the second, causing a matter/ anti-matter explosion.

"One ship left in sensor range," Daniel says.

"Levi, overtake them." She commands. "Sacar, fire at will." Within seconds the ship is destroyed.

"Long range sensors clear," Daniel tells his wife.

• • •

"Good," She says, turning to Fental. "Not now," She tells her first officer before she can speak. "Tell Benjamin I need to know how badly damaged we are this time."

"Right away, captain." He says.

Several minutes go by and he turbolift door opens. Benjamin steps onto the bridge and approaches the captain.

"What's the good word?" She asks him with a polite smile.

"The hull breaches on the upper drive section," He begins. "The other systems are up and running but hull repair, that's something else."

"What do you need from me?" The captain asks.

"How about six days in dock?" He suggests.

"That's not going to happen." She replies, keeping her smile wide and bright.

"I don't know what else to say, captain. We need material and time."

"How about this?" She starts. "Keep us together until the remaining enemy ships are destroyed and I'm in command of the quadrant, then you'll have time to repair her properly,"

"Or what?" He asks.

"An airlock," She says. "How's that?"

"Understood," He replies with a look of shock. Give us three hours."

"Good, get back to work." Her smile never wavering as he leaves the bridge, angry and confused.

"Captain," Fental says with slight harshness. Atany shoots her a look, behind her smile, that sends a shiver down Fental's spine. "I'm going to get a coffee." He says with forced calmness. "Would you like one?"

"Thank you but no." Atany replies. Fental stands, stretches and heads to the aft corridor. Hawking follows behind her. The two walk to the mess hall together. They sit in the corner furthest from all the other occupied tables.

"She's lost it," Fental says showing anger.

"Shh," Hawking replies. "Keep your voice down, to below a whisper."

"She's lost it," Fental repeats somewhat quieter.

"I know."

"Now she's threatening the crew."

"I know."

"And Benjamin has been chief engineer before Atany even got here."

"I know."

"Well what the hell are we going to do about it?"

"I don't know."

Fental's face distorts with the confusion of realizing the content of the current conversation. They both start laughing.

"Sorry," She says. "Too much freakin' stress."

"Don't worry about it. I know the feeling."

"But seriously, what are we going to do?"

"We need to get off of this ship without getting killed," He starts. "The only way to do that is to leave when no one is paying attention."

"The only time everyone is distracted enough for us to get away is when we're under attack." She mentions to him.

"Then we have to leave during combat," Hawking states.

"That's gonna be just as dangerous," She replies.

"That all depends," He answers partially lost in thought. "During our next battle, when there are, let's say, four enemy ships left, we get to the *Deliverance* and leave. We can avoid the enemy while Sacar destroys them and get out of sensor range before Daniel focuses on us."

"We'd have to time it out just right or we're dead," She reminds him.

"We'll have to discretely find any others interested in bugging out of here," He adds.

"Are you talking about mutiny?" Lieutenant Jasmine says quietly and quickly as she approached their table from somewhere.

"What the fuck!" Fental says with surprise. "You scared the shit out of me." She lets out a sigh of relief.

"And for the record, we're not talking about mutiny." Hawking says. "That kind of talk can get you killed."

"I know," Jasmine admits as she sits with them. "What happened with Benjamin freaked me out. I just want to get away from here alive. If the Alliance and the Utorians don't destroy this ship, some group, somewhere will be trying. I don't want to be around here went it happens."

"We're talking about escape, not about taking over," Aristotle repeats.

"Good, taking over would be way too difficult." Jasmine says.

"Did you hear what we were saying?" Fental asks her.

"Only part of it," She answers. "Something about stealing the *Deliverance* when there are four enemy ships left."

"Yes," Fental clarifies. "During the next battle, when you see us leave the bridge, follow."

"Great," Jasmine says with a smile. "I'll grab my Ex Vee. With two ships we'll double our chances of escape."

"We've got to get back to the bridge before Atany thinks something's up," Fental says after a few minutes.

"You two go," Hawking says. "I've got one stop to make first."

"What if Atany asks?" Fental asks.

"Tell her you don't know where I am."

"Where are you going?"

"I'll be back soon."

"You're not going to tell me, are you?"

"I don't want you lying to the captain."

"Understood," Fental answers as Jasmine looks on in confusion. The three leave the mess hall, Fental and Jasmine going forward and Hawking walks aft.

Hawking returns to the bridge thirty minutes after Fental and Jasmine.

"Is everything alright?" Atany asks.

"Yeah, fine," Hawking replies. "Why do you ask?"

"Just curious," The captain answers.

"Had to use the toilet," He responds.

"Ahh," Is Atany's only reply as Aristotle sits at his station.

While Benjamin and the rest of the engineering crew not on duty continue with the repairs, Daniel, Hawking and Sacar scan around the ship as it cruises through space at full impulse power.

"Nothing, captain," Daniel says after an hour.

"That's okay," Atany answers. "We'll find them. We'll find them and destroy them all. We still have a couple of hours, at least."

"Levi, plot a course that brings us within scanning range of the asteroid field and the nebula."

"What are you thinking?" Daniel asks.

"Checking the most obvious hiding places for a fleet as large as we're looking for," She replies.

"Very good," Fental says, smiling to cover the repulsion she now feels for Atany.

As time passes, the bridge remains silent as everyone performs their duties in anticipation of the coming battle. Time ticks by slowly as nothing is showing on the sensors. Fatigue sets in quickly as the tension of anticipation stretches over the long minutes.

The second hour passes as the first one did. All systems are patched and at one hundred percent, but no one can be certain how long they will function under pressure. All that remains is the structural uncertainties.

"We'll be in sensor range of the Danarus asteroid field in ten minutes," Levi tells the captain.

"Excellent," She replies. The ten minutes feel more like an hour.

"Starting scans of the asteroid field," Daniel says.

"Same here," Hawking adds. Another ten minutes pass.

● ● ●

"Captain," Benjamin's voice blares on the bridge.

"Atany, here."

"We've got the drive section as secure as possible," He says. "We've reinforced the area with force fields. It's as good as it gonna get."

"Understood," She answers. "Good job."

With the news of the repairs being complete, morale is up and everyone is focused on staying alive. Five hours pass without any contact. The *Tartarus* makes its way from the asteroid field to the Rhinehart nebula at warp two.

"Levi, bring us around to the far side of the nebula and hold us there." Atany orders. The big ship maneuvers around the massive gas cloud and parks on the far side.

"Daniel, put an overview of the quadrant on the screen." Commands Atany and the main viewscreen flickers as the image changes from the static star pattern and gaseous nebula to the quadrant overview.

The planets are displayed with their names. The asteroid field and nebula are there as well. A blue dot blinking by the nebula denotes the Forzak battlecruiser.

"What's on your mind, captain?" Fental asks.

"Well," She starts with a look of concern. "If I were in command of a fleet, where would I want to rendezvous to plan an attack?" Everyone on the bridge, hearing the captain's question, concentrate on the viewscreen, hoping to be the one with the right answer.

"Let's break it down," Daniel says.

"How do you mean?" Fental asks.

"Hawking, can you remove Spaceport One and Research Station Alpha?"

"Sure," Hawking answers and the two markers, indicating the two space-stations, blink away.

"Since we destroyed them, there is no way a fleet can be there."

"I see," Atany says with a brightened outlook. "We can remove Horatha, Chandar Two, Rill and Utoria." The four dots blink out along with their names.

"Now get rid of the asteroid field and the nebula," Daniel adds and the two largest markers vanish. The screen looks barren with only a few dots remaining.

"Now remove H'Too Bar'klaa and Orancara Four." Hawking says as he deletes them.

"Now the Brantax system," Fental says with a hint of concern and it blinks away.

"Now, what systems are left that a fleet can use?" Atany asks.

"There's only Mylar and Zareth," Sacar chimes in. "And neither of them are advanced enough to assist yet."

"That would leave us with an easy answer," Daniel states. "None." They sit back in idle contemplation when Atany's eyes grow large and fear sweeps across her face.

"Get us into the nebula, now," Atany shouts. "Full impulse, now!"

The ship streaks along and, just as she is about to enter the nebula, the battlecruiser rocks violently.

"I've got fifteen ships at one, eight, zero mark three, three." Daniel reports. "Five hundred kilometers."

"Lock on to however many you can before the nebula interrupts your sensors and blow them up," Atany orders.

Volley after volley of torpedoes and phaser bolts flank the space between the *Tartarus* and the attacking force. By the time the enemy ships realize the scope of the assault seven have been destroyed and four are limping away damaged. The *Tartarus* takes damage as well but the repaired systems are holding together well.

As the ship enters the nebula, another series of volleys take out the four damaged ships. The remaining four ships warp away. The *Tartarus* escapes deep into the Rhinehart nebula.

"How did you know, captain?" Fental asks

• • •

"It's what I would have done." She replies.

"Done what?" Hawking asks, confused. "I don't get it."

"They were in the asteroid field," Atany answers.

"We scanned the field. They weren't there." He continues, still confused.

"They were *inside* the asteroids," Atany continues to explain. "Inside caverns and caves. Inside the asteroids, inside the field."

"Clever," Hawking responds.

"Where the fuck are the rest of them?" She asks aloud.

"You know, Atany," Daniel says after a few minutes. "We completely destroyed every planet's capability to destroy us… except one… the Brantax system. We were attacked before we could finish our assault."

"Fental reported that their capabilities to do us harm were destroyed," Atany tells him.

"What if the reports were inaccurate," He speculates.

"Are you calling me a liar?" Fental asks angrily as she stands and faces Daniel.

"Not at all," He replies. "There was a lot going on. It's possible the reports got mixed and you read the wrong one. A Simple mistake. I meant no disrespect."

"Alright, then," Fental answers, more relaxed. Inside, she is scared shitless at possibly giving herself away to the captain. She sits back in her seat.

"Levi, set a course for the Brantax system, warp seven." The captain commands.

"Aye, captain." He replies as he manipulates the controls on his console. "ETA two point six hours."

"Captain," Levi begins. "We are entering sensor range of the Brantax system."

"Anything on long range sensors?" Atany asks.

"Sensors clear," Daniel reports.

● ● ●

"They could be hiding behind any of the planets or moons within the system," Hawking reminds the bridge crew. "Stay alert. There are dozens of possible hiding spots."

The battlecruiser glides past the three moons of Brantax Eleven, entering orbit around the world they visited to find Hawking several months earlier.

"Scan the surface for any of the assault fleet," Atany orders.

"Scanning," Daniel repeats as he complies. It takes several minutes to complete the scan.

"There's nothing down there," Sacar tells her.

"Okay, let's move on to the next one." She commands.

"Setting course for Brantax Ten," Levi says. The ship cruises along at full impulse. The voyage takes two and a half minutes.

"Nothing here, either." Sacar tells the captain.

The ship moves from planet to planet, trying to locate and destroy the enemy fleet. Nothing is found on any of the worlds leading to Brantax Three, the only other planet besides Brantax Eleven that has life.

"I've got eight ships at the spaceport," Sacar says with enthusiasm. "Library computer shows them to be Utorian, all of them."

"Leaves about twenty-five unaccounted for, Atany says aloud to herself. "But let's take them when we can."

Sacar fires six volleys of weapon's fire toward the targets on the surface. It takes nearly two minutes for the death rain to reach their targets. Plumes caused by the explosions on the surface can be seen on the viewscreen. About thirty seconds pass.

"All eight ships have been destroyed," Sacar informs the captain.

"Good," Atany replies. "Now let's find the rest..." The rocking of the ship interrupts her. "Never mind," She continues. "I know where they are. Lock weapons on targets and fire!" Atany commands with authority.

The battlecruiser launches a massive barrage against the wall of enemy ships. Weapon's fire from the assault fleet passes the torpedoes fired by the *Tartarus*. As three of the Alliance warships turn into fireballs the Tartarus rocks hard side to side as consoles explode around the remaining bridge crew.

Smoke hangs low on the bridge as more consoles short out, sparks lighting the dimly lit room.

"Fire!" Atany shouts as five ships come into view on the screen. Phaser bolts and torpedoes speed toward the five ships and, one by one, they are vaporized in brilliant matter/ antimatter explosions.

The Forzak ship rolls hard right and banks left as phasers fire from the rear of the weapon's nacelles. Three more ships explode as a direct result of the phasers and torpedoes. A fourth ship explodes from debris impact.

More phaser fire impacts the *Tartarus*, causing the huge ship to rock. The lights flicker momentarily, causing panic to sweep throughout the ship. Fental and Hawking lock eyes, each reading the other's face.

The ship rocks once again as Fental gets up quickly and heads to the console by Hawking. She reaches the console and activates the controls. As the ship rocks again she inputs commands for the computer to begin prelaunch sequences on the *Deliverance* and Ex Vees. Atany doesn't notice.

"It'll take twenty minutes for the preflight checks," Fental tells Hawking when she finishes.

"We just have to make sure we're alive in twenty minutes," Hawking replies with a nervous smile.

The battle continues as the enemy fleet dwindles down in size and the Tartarus takes a beating.

"Engineering to bridge," Comes over the speakers on the bridge. "Hull breach in the upper drive section is open again. Force fields are holding but are at ninety-two percent."

"Understood," She replies and turns to the tactical station. "How many ships left?"

"Sensors reading sixteen left," Sacar reports.

"Four are heavily damaged and backing away," Hawking adds.

"Take out the remaining twelve," She commands. "We'll get those four afterward."

The viewscreen shows waves of phaser bolts and torpedoes flying back and forth between the Forzak battlecruiser and Alliance and Utorian warships.

Consoles explode in showers of brilliantly lit sparks all around the bridge as warships explode in fierce fireballs outside of the ship. A three man damage control team, led by Commander Benjamin, enters the bridge.

The three technicians head off to diagnose different consoles as Benjamin goes to the console beside Fental. He initializes the console and calls up the engineering controls.

"Forcefields covering the hull breach are at eighty-three percent," He informs the captain. She nods in acknowledgement. The battle continues as the technicians try to repair systems as they short out. The lights flicker, staying out for a longer duration.

"How many left?" Atany asks above the sounds of plasma leaks and systems shorting out and sparking.

"Six attacking, four retreating," He answers.

"Continue as you are doing," She tells him.

"Yes, ma'am," He replies. "Continuing assault." The viewscreen once again fills with phaser bolts and photon torpedoes. Utorian and Alliance ships alike explode under the assault.

"The four escaping Alliance ships are nearly out of sensor range," Daniel reports after several minutes.

"The three remaining Utorian ships are swinging around for another pass," Sacar says.

"Forcefields at seventy-four percent," Benjamin concludes the reports.

* * *

"Break off our attack and pursue the four escaping ships," She orders.

"Aye, captain." Levi says as the ship swings around ninety degrees and follows an intercept course to the crippled ships.

It takes four minutes to reach them while the last three Utorian ships fall behind in pursuit. The *Tartarus* reaches the Alliance ships while still in sensor range of the Utorian ships.

"I've got them now," She says as she leans forward in her chair, slyly grinning.

"Captain!" Daniel shouts with surprise and confusion.

"What?" She replies.

"Some kind of vortex is forming," He starts. "Starboard, aft, one hundred, thousand kilometers."

"On screen now," She orders. "Sacar, continue with the Alliance ships." The viewscreen changes, showing a black vortex surrounded by swirling clouds of plasma.

"What is that?" She asks with a puzzling look.

"Unknown," Daniel says. "The ship's memory bank contains a visual record of this same phenomenon, as well as collected data, but still concludes everything as unknown.

"Data shows something is coming through," Daniel continues and, as he finishes, the metallic edge of a ship can be seen at the edge of the darkness within the void.

The ship emerging through the vortex is of immense size. It is one and a half times longer than the *Tartarus* with five equal sides. Its main body is five decks high, coming to a point in the front.

There is a smaller, three deck high-riser above the main hull, flat in the front with a single window, presumably the bridge. On top of that there is a dome, lit from the inside. Behind the dome is a section, two decks high, that runs to the back of the vessel. Behind it are two engine exhaust ports.

The belly of the ship has a glowing circle at the five corners. They too are glowing. In the center is a pentagonal hatch. As the unknown ship fully immerges from the vortex, the hatch slowly opens. Once it finishes opening, a long shaft, with a cone-shaped crystal tip, slowly emerges. It starts to glow, dimly at first but glowing brighter by the second.

"Oh fuck," Sacar say in astonishment. "Oh, Gods, no!" Fear taking over as his eyes grow wider.

"What is it, Sacar?" Atany asks. "You recognize that ship?" Before he could answer, the cone-shaped glowing crystal fires a beam of florescent, blue plasma at one of the advancing Utorian warships, cleanly slicing it in half.

"Yes, captain," Sacar continues. "We encountered a ship of that design on our mission to Terra. It's Nephillium!" Distress fills his words. "Only this one is at least ten times bigger." A second beam fires from the ship, slicing another Utorian ship in half. The third ship swings around.

"Captain," Roeton says. "We are being hailed." A solemn quiet envelopes the bridge.

"On screen," She says. The image of a being appears on the viewscreen. It is tall with spindly arms and legs. Its head is disproportionably large with large oval eyes. It appears to have no gender.

"I am Karam Ra, Partner to Takal Ra." The being says in a strangely hypnotic voice. "When our sensors registered the activation of the first vortex, we recognized it as a rekindling of a distant memory. When we arrived at the dead world and scanned your ship, imagine our surprise when we found it was the same ship that interfered with our experiment at the far side of the galaxy, as did the race that built the ship you now possess. We destroyed them as we will destroy you."

"I think now would be a good time to leave," Hawking tells Fental.

"I think you're right," She acknowledges and the two quietly leave the bridge. Jasmine, seeing the two leave, quickly follows. Benjamin follows behind the three.

"He's talking about Terra, captain." Sacar clarifies.

"I am Captain Dinema Atany of the *Tartarus*," Atany tells him. "I wasn't at Terra, I can't speak for what went on there."

"But some of your crew were, by the sound of it." Karam Ra says with little emotion.

"I was assigned to the *Heaven* after Jehovah returned from the mission to Terra," She reaffirms.

"That is of no consequence," His voice expelling a little anger. "After your species destroyed our experiment on what you call Terra, your captain, that ship, nearly decimated my civilization. We were caught off guard, in a sneak attack." His anger becomes more pronounced. "The dishonor… the disrespect, your captain, your species exercised, demonstrated to us the need for your extinction."

"What the hell are you talking about? Our extinction?" Atany says with contempt. "Think again, fucker." She turns to Sacar as the screen's image goes back to the Nephillium starship. The cone-shaped crystal starts glowing brighter as the Nephillium ship prepares to fire.

"Brace for impact!" Atany yells and at that moment the last Utorian ship fires at the alien starship, causing it to rock to the left. The beam fires from the crystal. The lights flash as consoles explodes around the bridge.

"Captain," Comes over the armrest intercom. "The upper hull assembly above the drive section, the one with the hull breaches, has been blasted away."

The hanger deck hatch opens and the four run in as the lights flash several times. Fental and Hawking head for the *Deliverance* as Jasmine runs toward her Ex Vee. Benjamin heads for the other Ex Vee.

"You can't take that," Jasmine tells him. "You haven't been trained in how to fly that."

"Don't worry," He says with a smile. "I'll figure it out. I'm an engineer, it's what I do."

The two climb aboard the fighters as Fental and Hawking secure the modified transport. The inner doors start to open as the power fails. It takes just under a minute for the power to return and the doors continue to open.

The *Deliverance* is the first to drop out, followed by Jasmine, in Ex Vee Four, then Benjamin, in Ex Vee One. They streak along the under-belly and clear the battlecruiser at the engine exhaust ports. The transport heads out, at full impulse, directly behind the Forzak battlecruiser as Jasmine pulls her Ex Vee slightly to the right. Benjamin veers left, right into a phaser beam fired at the Nephillium ship by the *Tartarus*.

The fighter and the freighter speed silently into the night, leaving the battle behind them.

"Course, captain?" Hawking asks Fental with a smile.

"The Forzak homeworld sounds good to me. How about you?" She smiles back.

"Sounds good to me." He replies and goes about plotting a course to the coordinates so they can activate the Forzak vortex.

"*Deliverance* to Ex Vee Four," Fental says into the communications panel, using the Forzak communications array.

"Ex Vee Four here," Jasmine answers.

"How would you like to visit the Forzak homeworld?" Fental asks.

"I'd like it fine," She replies.

"Then follow us."

"Will do."

The conduits running along the ceiling of the bridge come crashing down, sending bellows of hot gases spewing around the command deck. The lights go out and, after a minute, the bridge is bathed in red light. The viewscreen blanks out and comes back in distorted flashes.

"What's our status?" Atany screams above the noise.

"Shields down to five percent," Daniel reports.

"Sacar, Fire all batteries," The captain yells in disgust. "Blow those fuckers up!"

The *Tartarus* fires three volleys from all available weapons ports. As the wall of destruction heads toward the Nephillium ship, two of the damaged Alliance warships fly between the two massive ships, absorbing nearly all the firepower launched by the *Tartarus*. They explode in huge fireballs.

The viewscreen flickers and Karam Ra is now looking at the remnants of the Forzak bridge. Atany shoots Daniel a look of desperation then faces the viewscreen.

"Captain Atany," Karam Ra says, once again with little emotion. "I want you to know, captain, when I finish you as I finished the Forzak Empire, I will destroy every living thing in the quadrant. When we have killed everything, we will start over and seed all the habitable worlds. We are a patient people, captain. We allowed you to see us in a way your species could understand. The Nephillium are forever, Dinema Atany, but you are not."

Atany runs to Daniel as the viewscreen flickers back to show the Nephillium ship, its crystal glows brightly. The captain and her husband lock their lips in a lover's embrace.

The Nephillium ship fires its deadly blue beam. It rips across the hull of the Tartarus, piercing through the body of the ship. The explosion of the Tartarus is so massive that the last two Alliance warships are destroyed by the shockwave. The unnamed Nephillium ship maneuvers around the debris and slowly makes its way to fulfill the promise made by its captain.

About the Author

Born in 1963, R.N. Chevalier has been a fan of all sci-fi from an early age. Inspired by the moon landing unfolding before him, he became an instant fan, seeing fantasy become reality. This inspiration came to fruition with the release of his first novel, *Are We the Klingons,* followed by *Advances of the Ancients. Full Circle* is the third book in the trilogy, based on a board game invented by the author.

www.ingramcontent.com/pod-product-compliance
Lightning Source LLC
Chambersburg PA
CBHW071247210626
46818CB00013B/420